LINTY

A POCKETFUL OF ADVENTURE

To Yasemin Uçar and Naseem Hrab, who joined me on this adventure as we shaped my first book into this fun little story that readers will hopefully enjoy day after day after day afterdayafterdayafterday ... well, you get the point — M.S.

Published in Canada and the U.S. by Kids Can Press Ltd.
25 Dockside Drive, Toronto, ON M5A 0B5

Kids Can Press is a Corus Entertainment Inc. company

www.kidscanpress.com

The artwork in this book was rendered in Staedtler 2B pencil and Photoshop.
The text is set in Hunniwell and Atma.

Edited by Yasemin Uçar
Designed by Michael Reis

Printed and bound in Shenzhen, China, in 10/2021 by C & C Offset

CM 22 0 9 8 7 6 5 4 3 2 1

FSC
www.fsc.org
MIX
Paper from
responsible sources
FSC® C008047

Library and Archives Canada Cataloguing in Publication

Title: Linty : a pocketful of adventure / Mike Shiell.
Names: Shiell, Mike, author, artist.
Identifiers: Canadiana 20210217227 | ISBN 9781525304941 (hardcover)
Subjects: LCGFT: Graphic novels.
Classification: LCC PN6733.S52 L56 2022 | DDC j741.5/971 — dc23

Kids Can Press gratefully acknowledges that the land on which our office is located is the traditional territory of many nations, including the Mississaugas of the Credit, the Anishnabeg, the Chippewa, the Haudenosaunee and the Wendat peoples, and is now home to many diverse First Nations, Inuit and Métis peoples.

We thank the Government of Ontario, through Ontario Creates; the Ontario Arts Council; the Canada Council for the Arts; and the Government of Canada for supporting our publishing activity.

LINTY

A POCKETFUL OF ADVENTURE

Mike Shiell

KIDS CAN PRESS

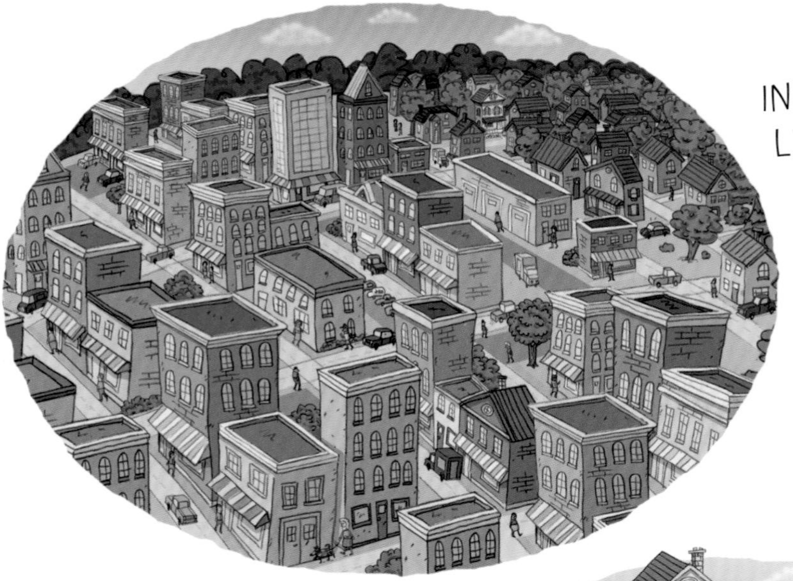

IN A SUNNY AND
LIVELY TOWN ...

ON A GREEN AND
LEAFY STREET ...

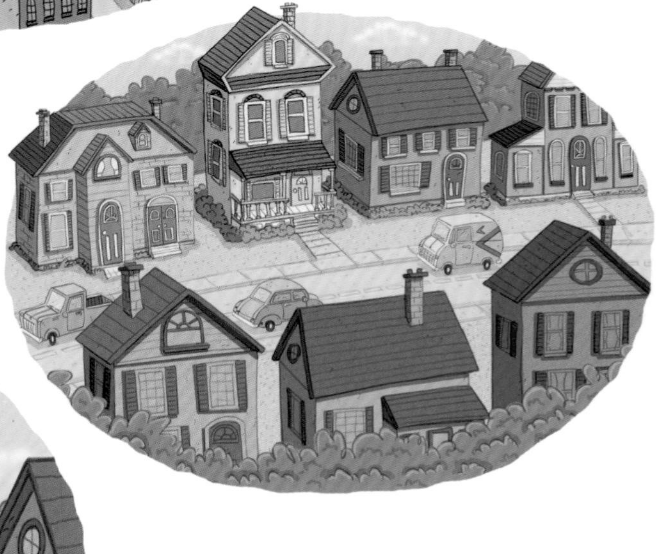

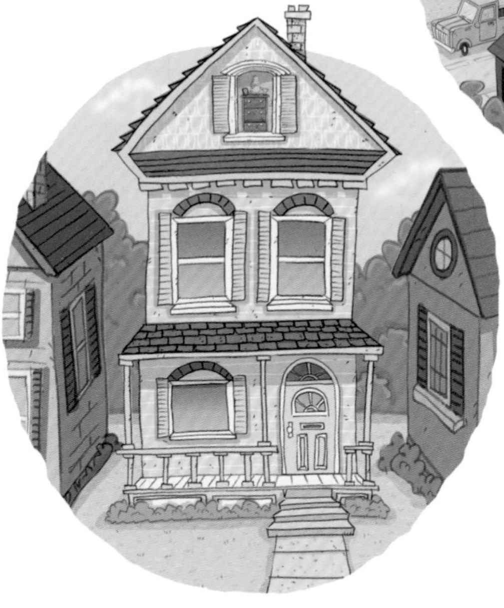

IN A PINK AND BLUE HOUSE ...

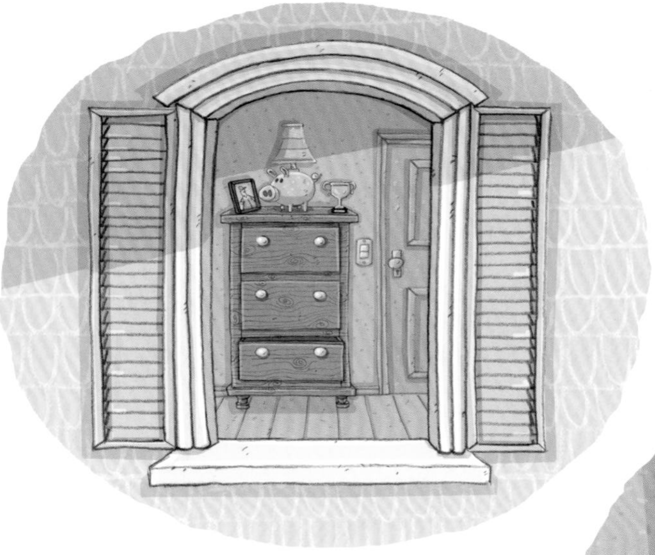

IN A BRIGHT AND
COMFY BEDROOM ...

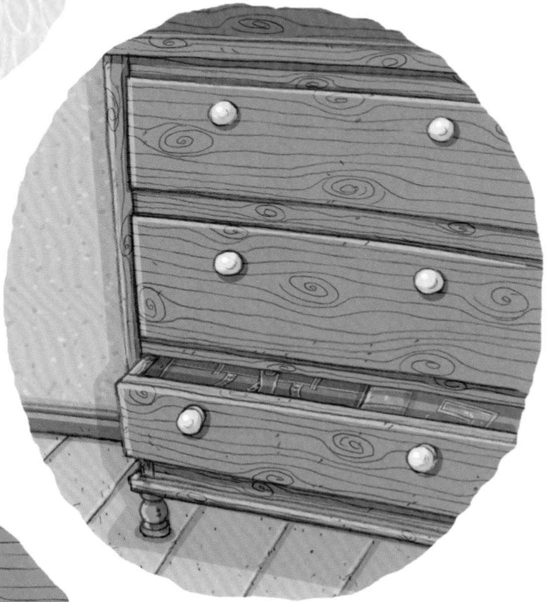

IN THE BOTTOM
DRAWER OF A LITTLE
BROWN DRESSER ...

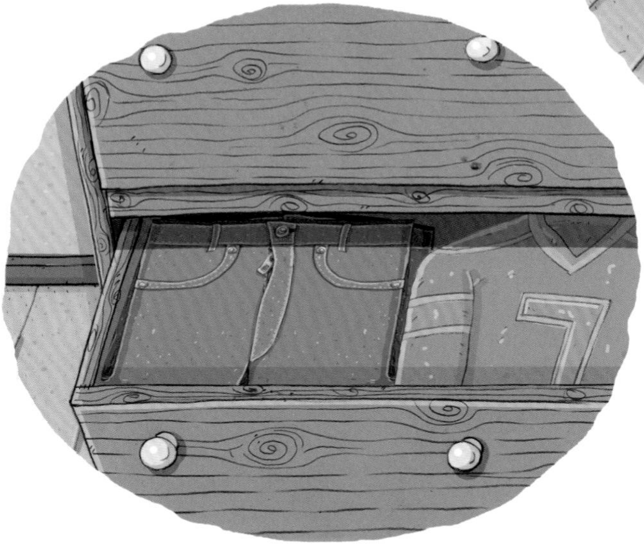

SNUGGLED IN THE
FRONT POCKET OF A
FADED PAIR OF JEANS ...

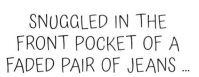

A TINY BALL OF LINT WOKE UP TO A NEW DAY.

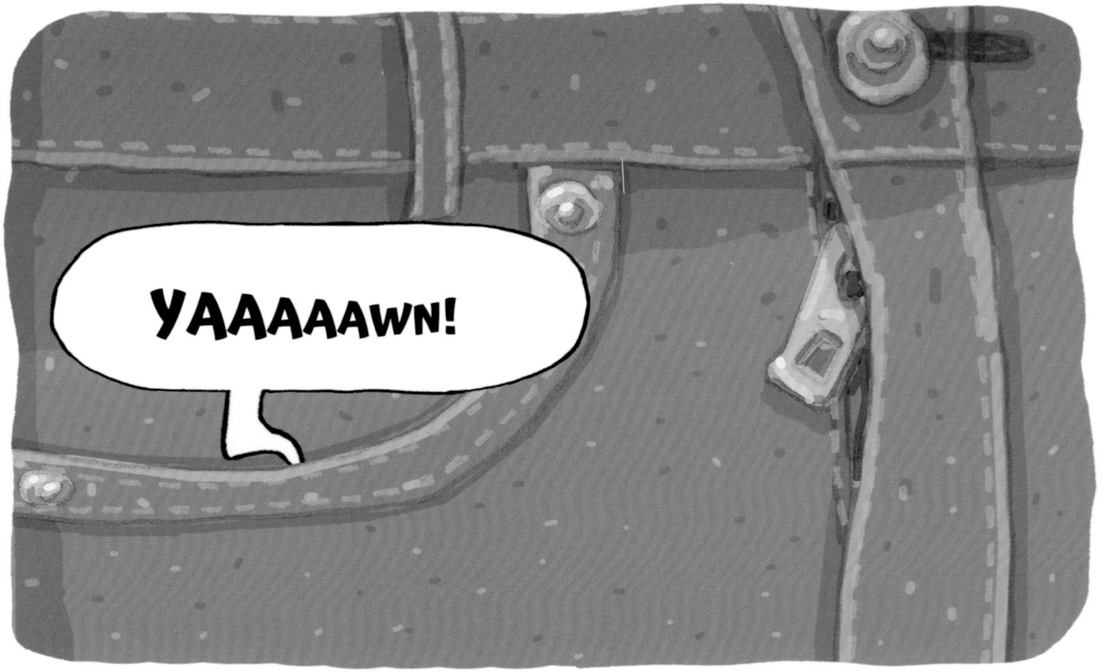
YAAAAAWN!

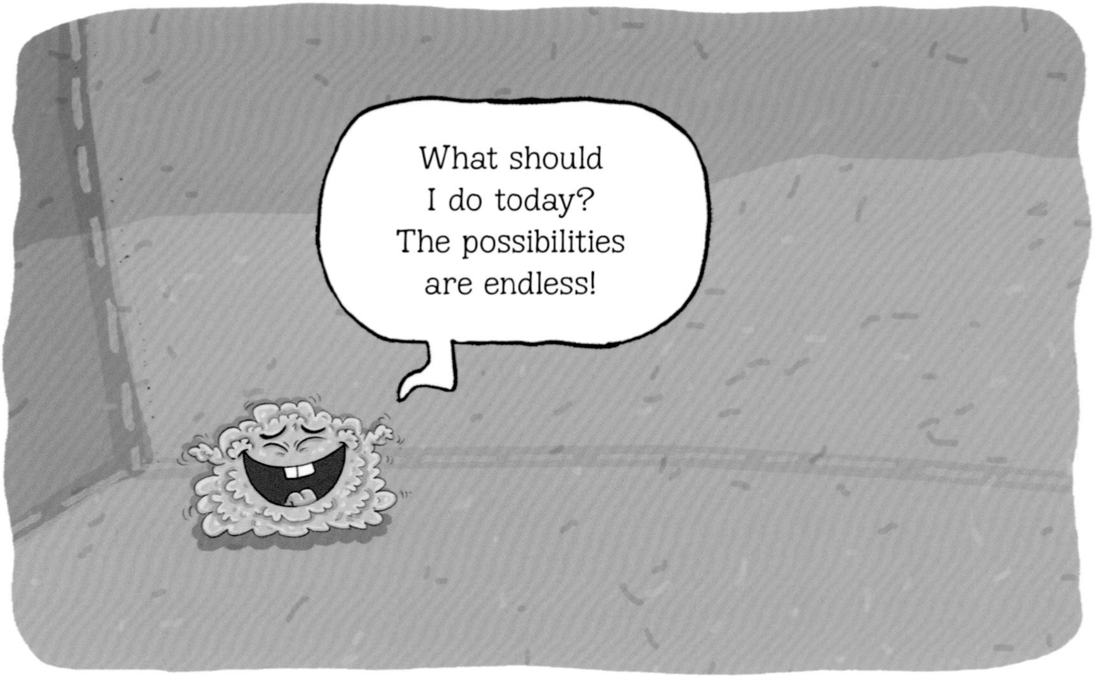
What should I do today? The possibilities are endless!

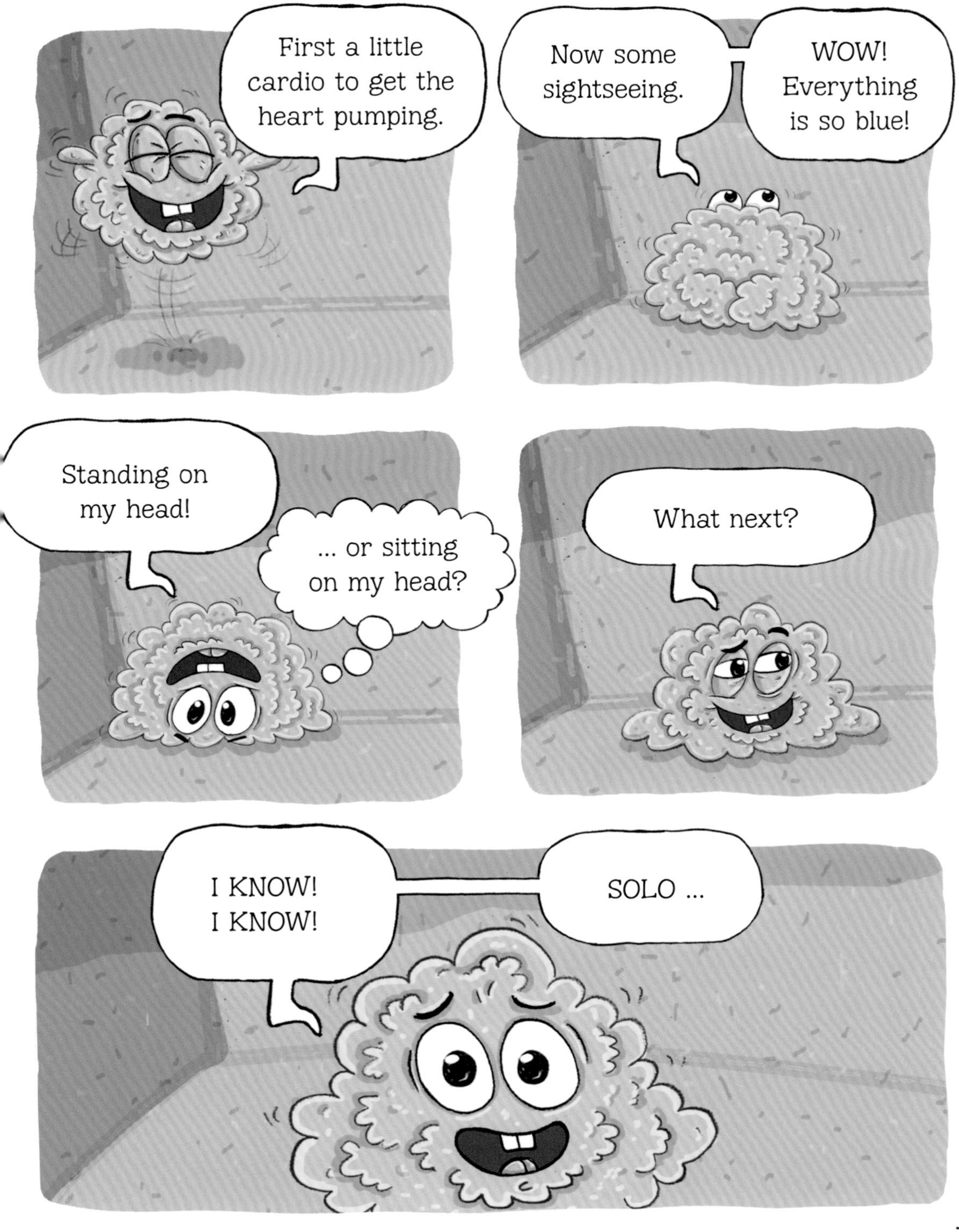
First a little cardio to get the heart pumping.
Now some sightseeing.
WOW! Everything is so blue!
Standing on my head!
... or sitting on my head?
What next?
I KNOW! I KNOW!
SOLO ...

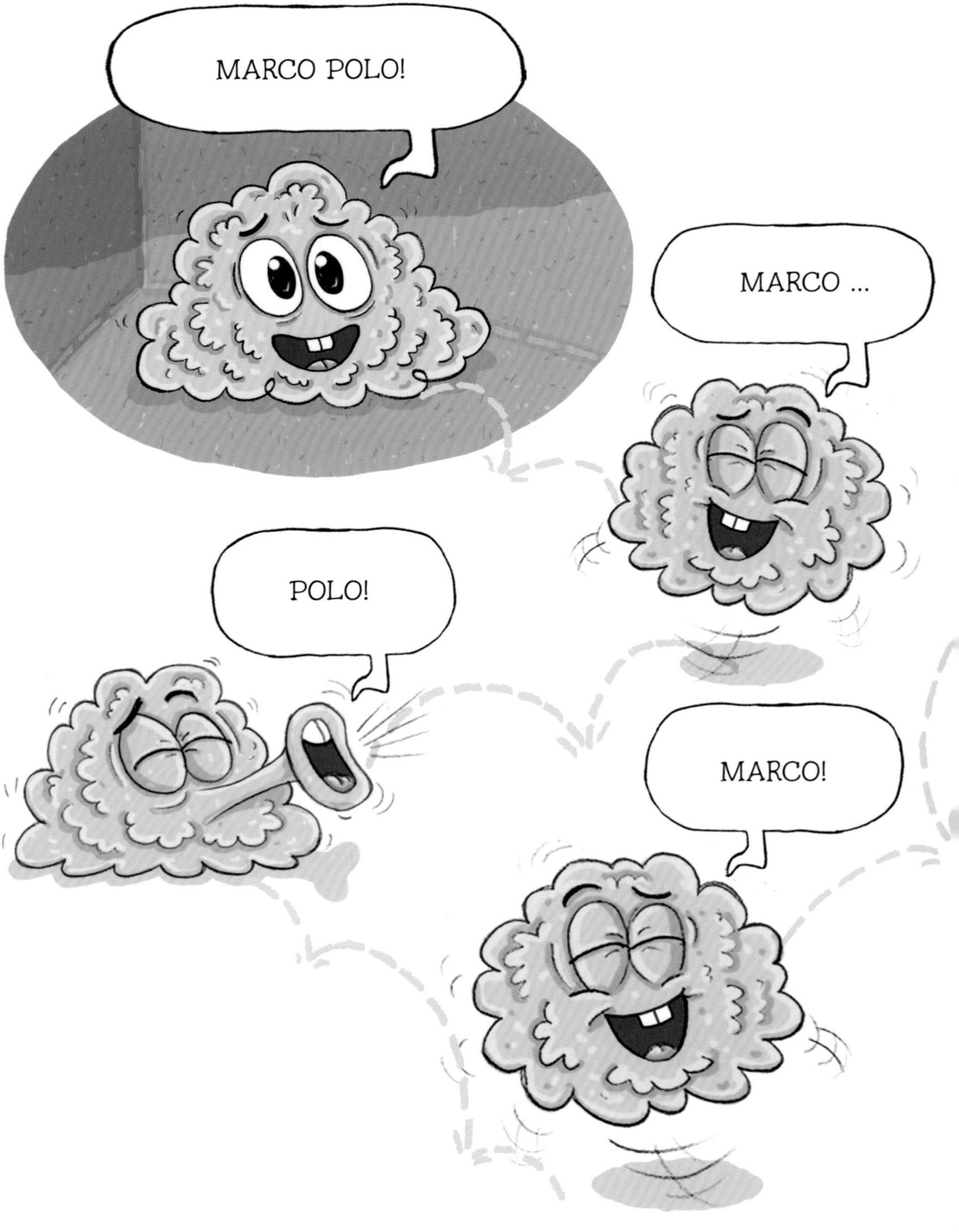
MARCO POLO!
MARCO ...
POLO!
MARCO!

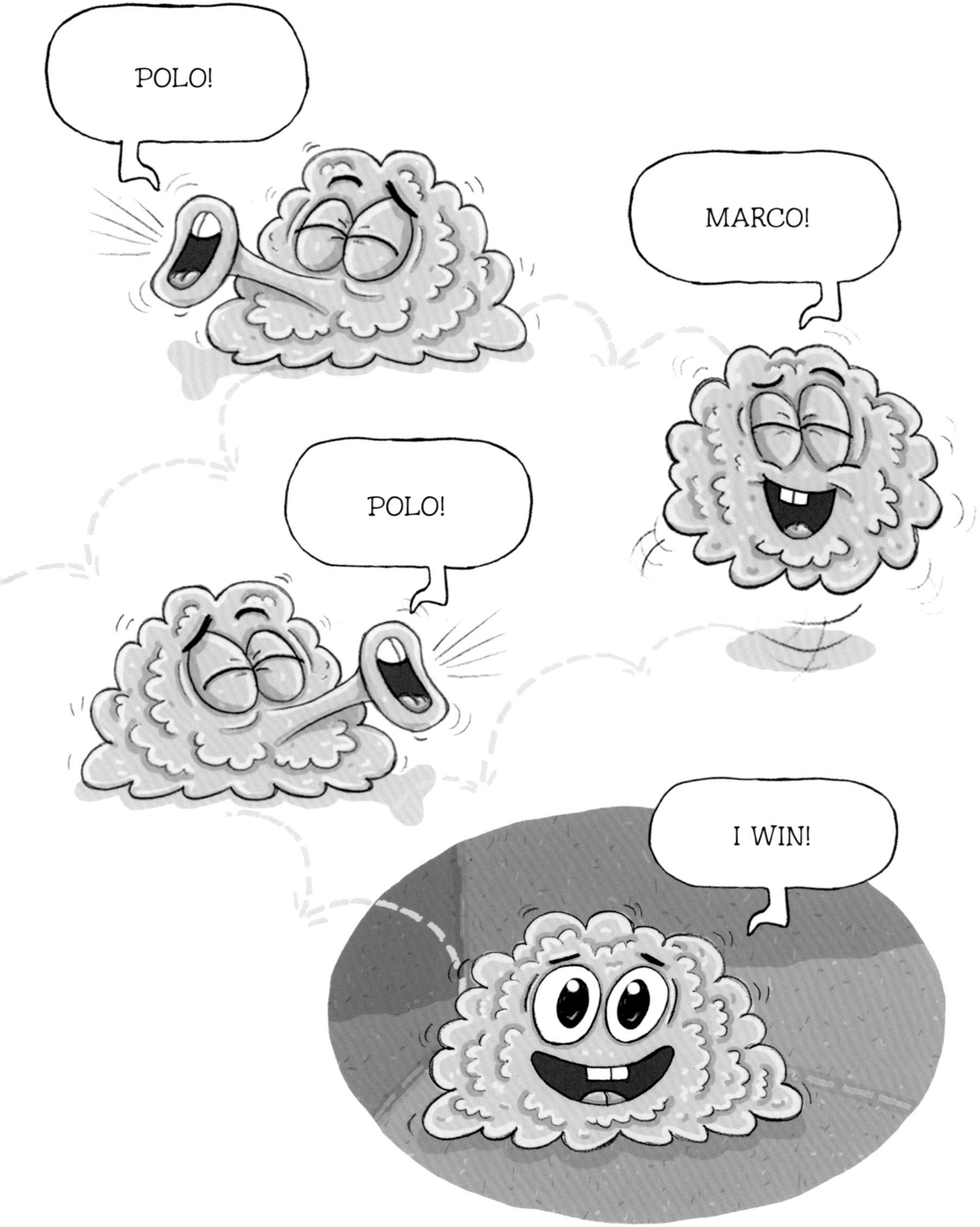
POLO!
MARCO!
POLO!
I WIN!

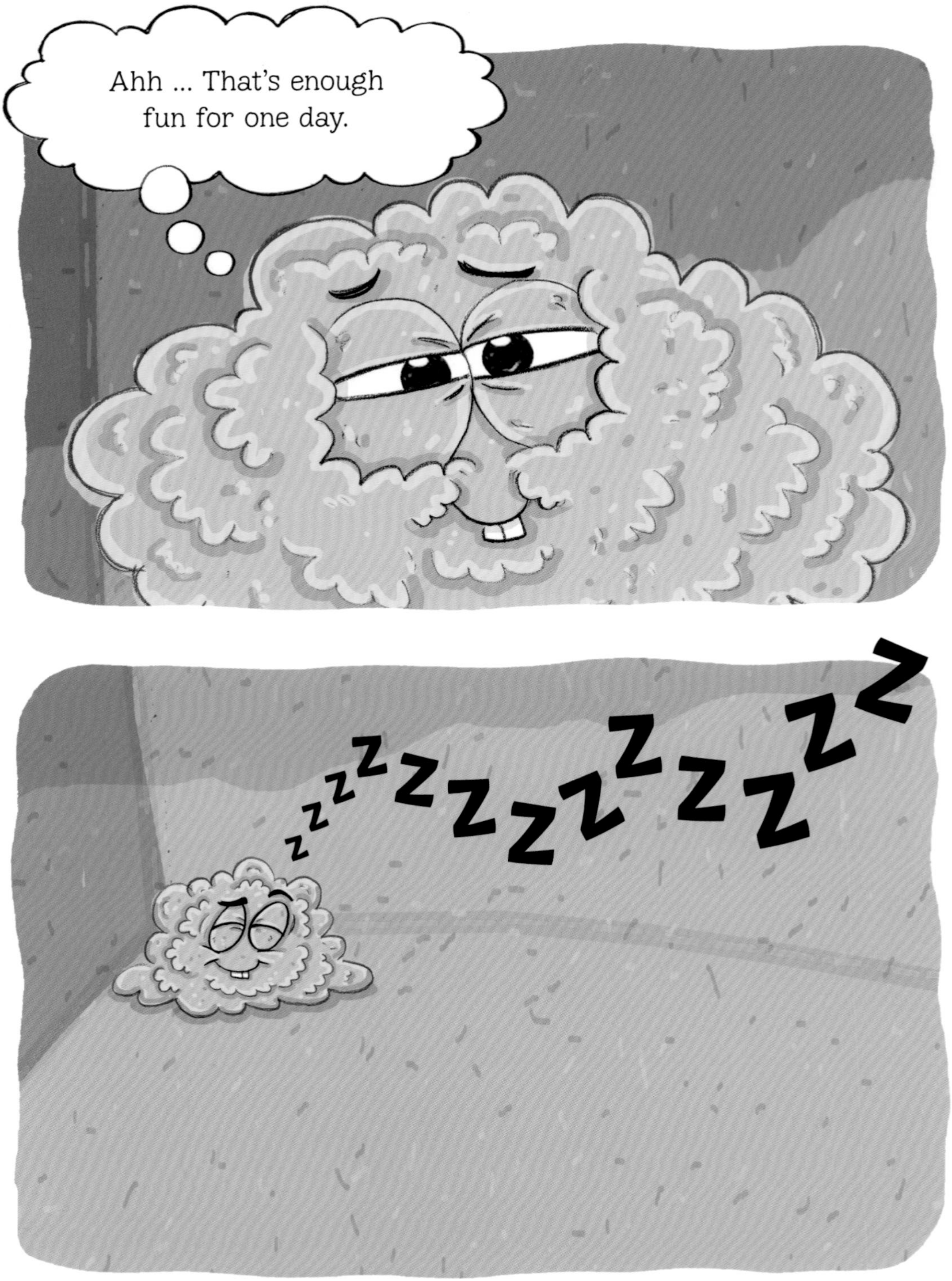
Ahh ... That's enough fun for one day.
zzzzZZZZZZZZZZ

IT WAS THE SAME DAY AFTER DAY AFTER DAY AFTER DAY AFTERDAYAFTERDAYAFTERDAYAFTER ... WELL, YOU GET THE POINT.

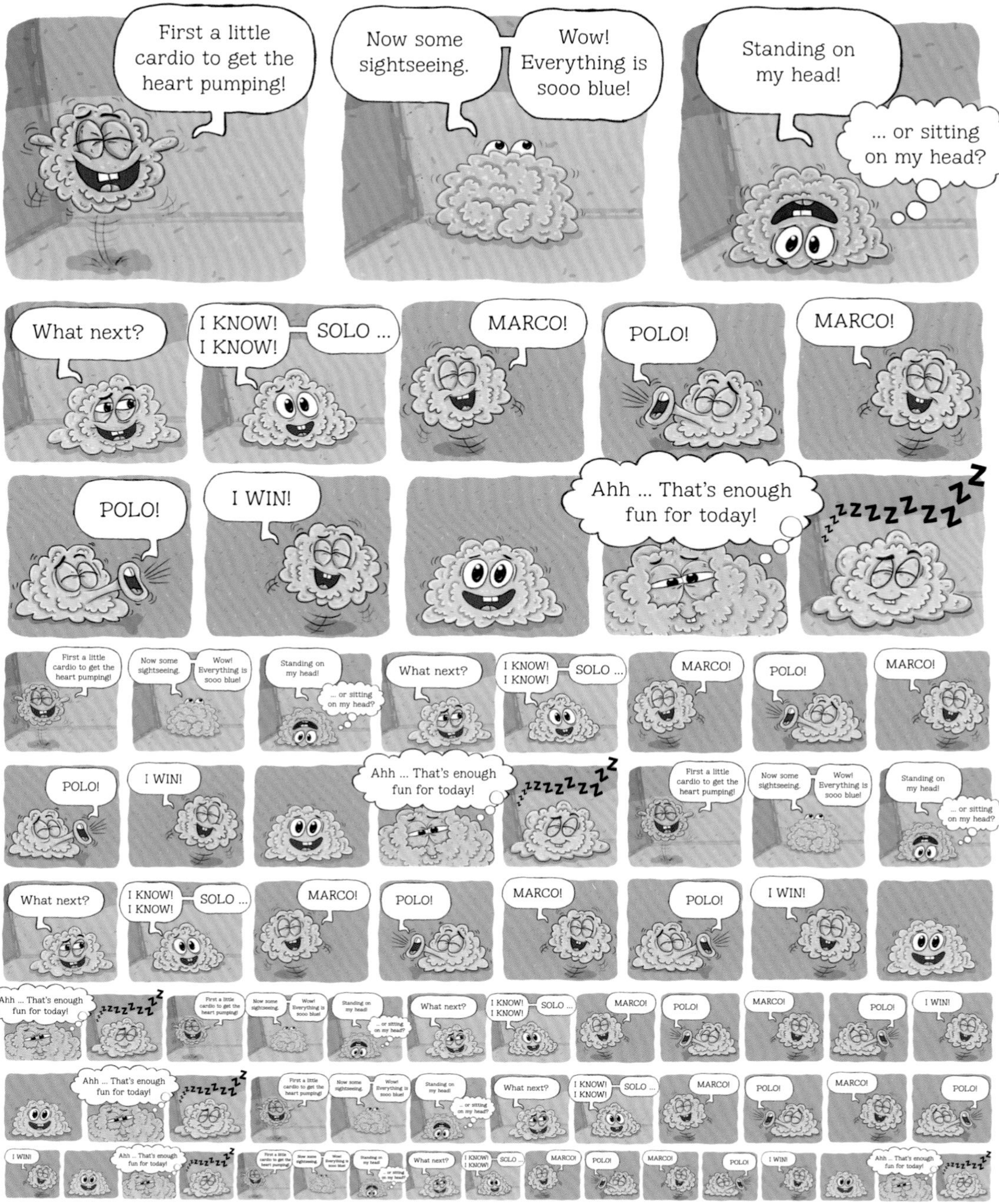

First a little cardio to get the heart pumping!
Now some sightseeing.
Wow! Everything is sooo blue!
Standing on my head!
... or sitting on my head?
What next?
I KNOW! I KNOW!
SOLO ...
MARCO!
POLO!
MARCO!
POLO!
I WIN!
Ahh ... That's enough fun for today!
First a little cardio to get the heart pumping!
Now some sightseeing.
Wow! Everything is sooo blue!
Standing on my head!
... or sitting on my head?
What next?
I KNOW! I KNOW!
SOLO ...
MARCO!
POLO!
MARCO!
POLO!
I WIN!
Ahh ... That's enough fun for today!
First a little cardio to get the heart pumping!
Now some sightseeing.
Wow! Everything is sooo blue!
Standing on my head!
... or sitting on my head?
What next?
I KNOW! I KNOW!
SOLO ...
MARCO!
POLO!
MARCO!
POLO!
I WIN!
Ahh ... That's enough fun for today!
What next?
I KNOW! I KNOW!
SOLO ...
MARCO!
POLO!
MARCO!
POLO!
I WIN!
Ahh ... That's enough fun for today!
What next?
I KNOW! I KNOW!
SOLO ...
MARCO!
POLO!
MARCO!
POLO!
I WIN!
Ahh ... That's enough fun for today!

UNTIL, ONE DAY, EVERYTHING CHANGED.

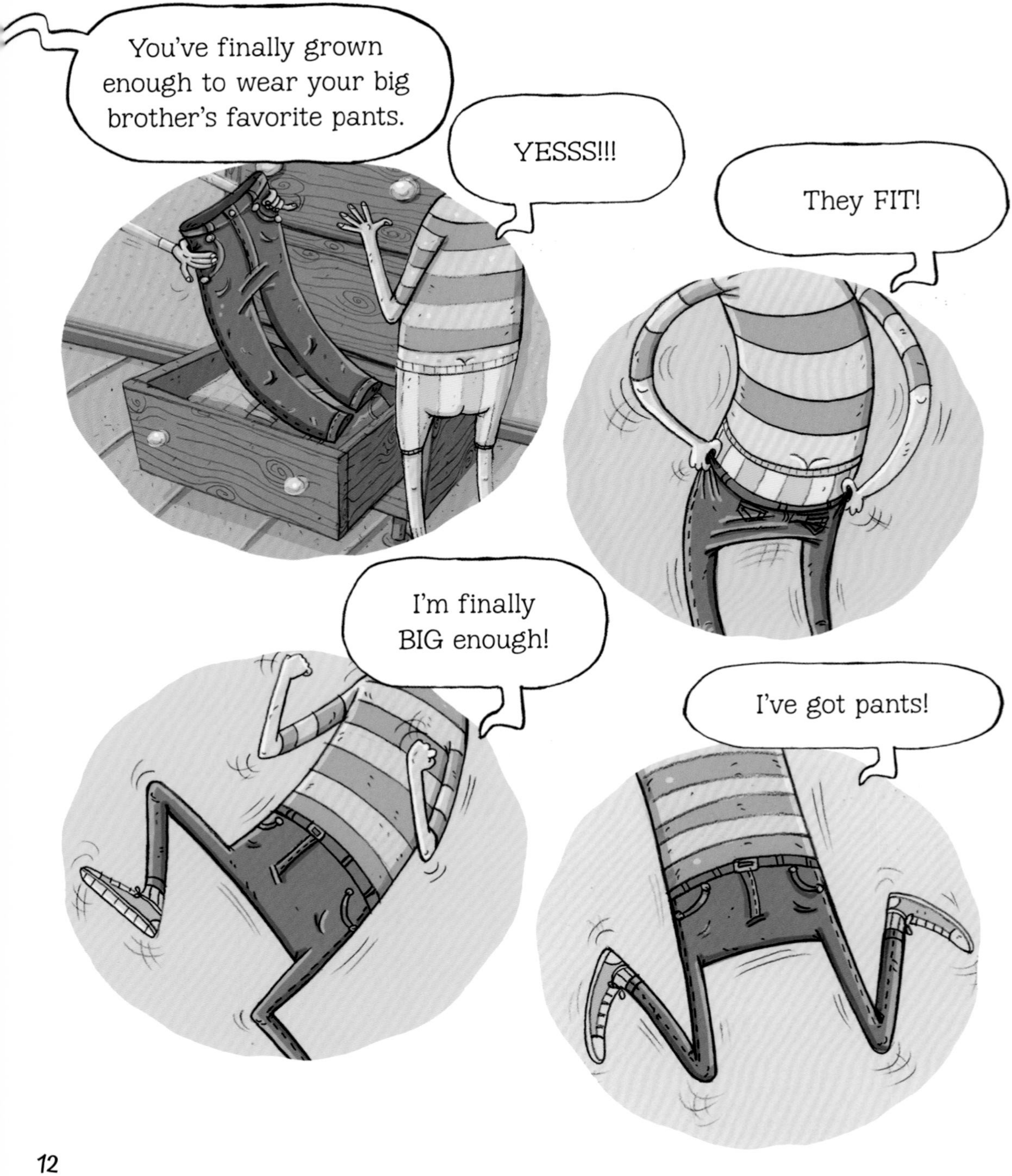
You've finally grown enough to wear your big brother's favorite pants.
YESSS!!!
They FIT!
I'm finally BIG enough!
I've got pants!

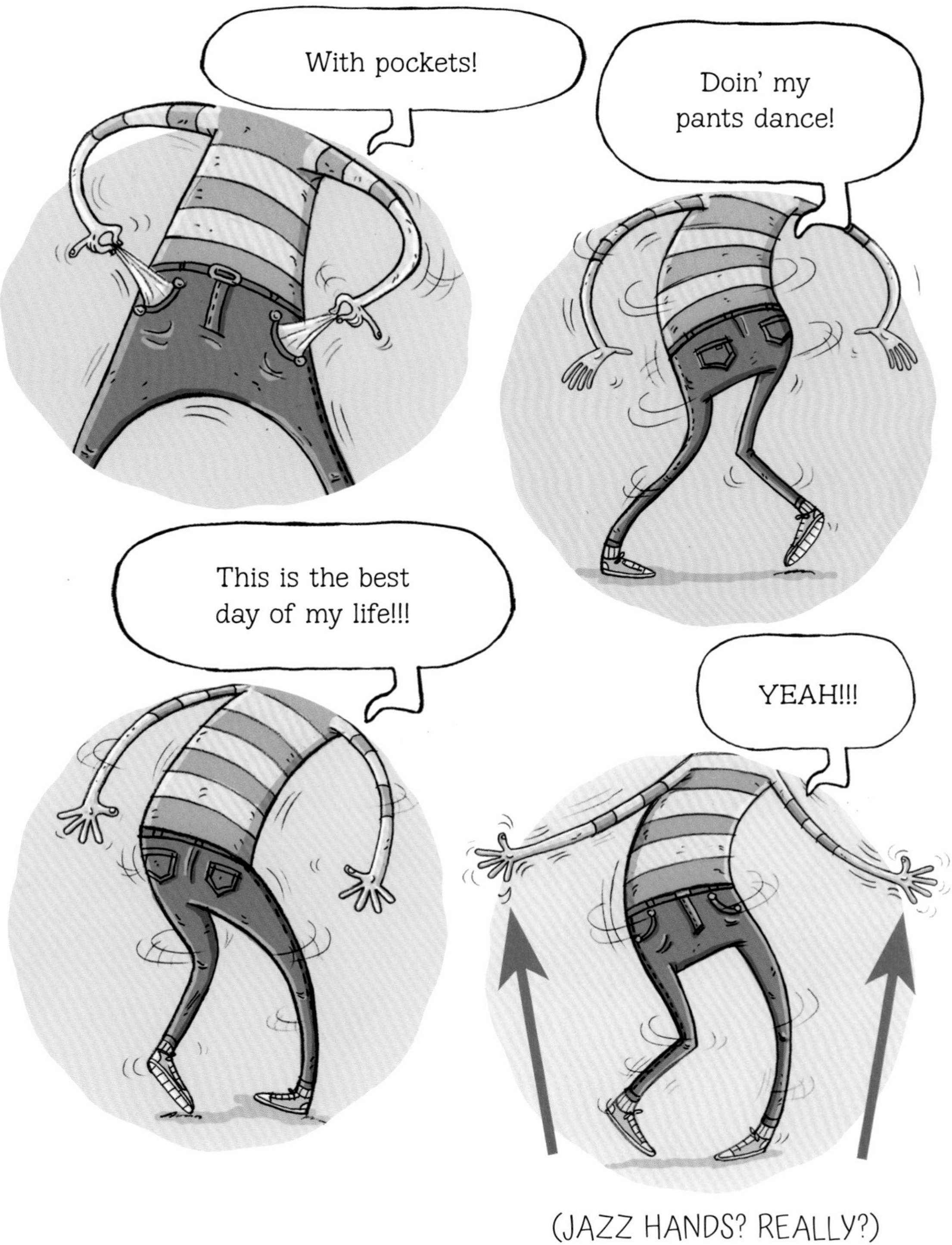
With pockets!
Doin' my pants dance!
This is the best day of my life!!!
YEAH!!!
(JAZZ HANDS? REALLY?)

ALL OF A SUDDEN, THE LITTLE BALL OF LINT STARTED TO MOVE AND RATTLE AND BOUNCE AND SHAKE AND JIGGLE.

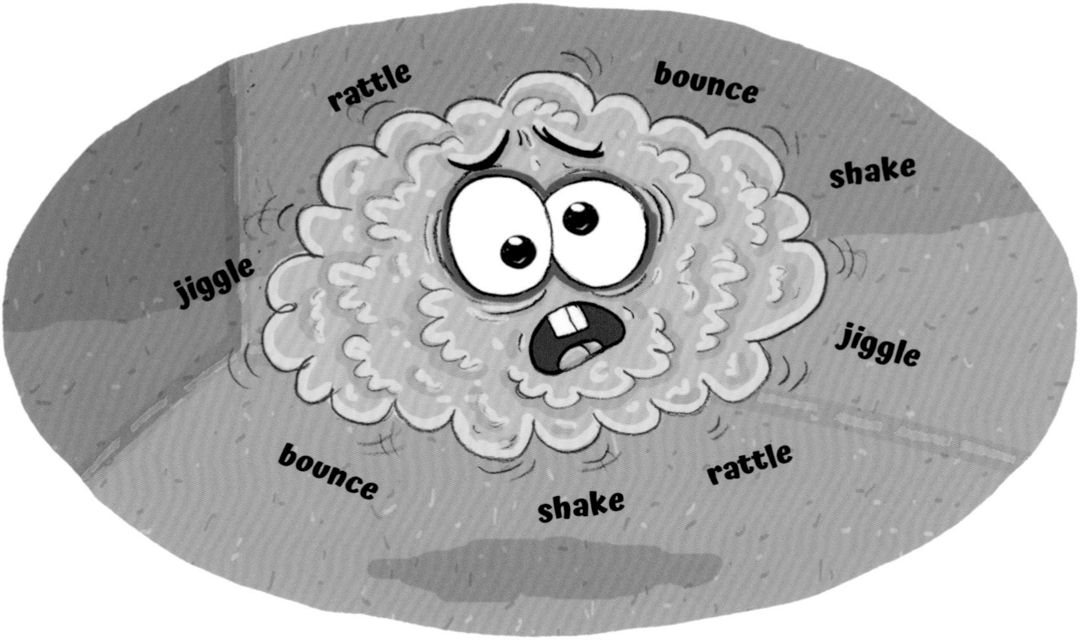
rattle
bounce
shake
jiggle
jiggle
bounce
shake
rattle

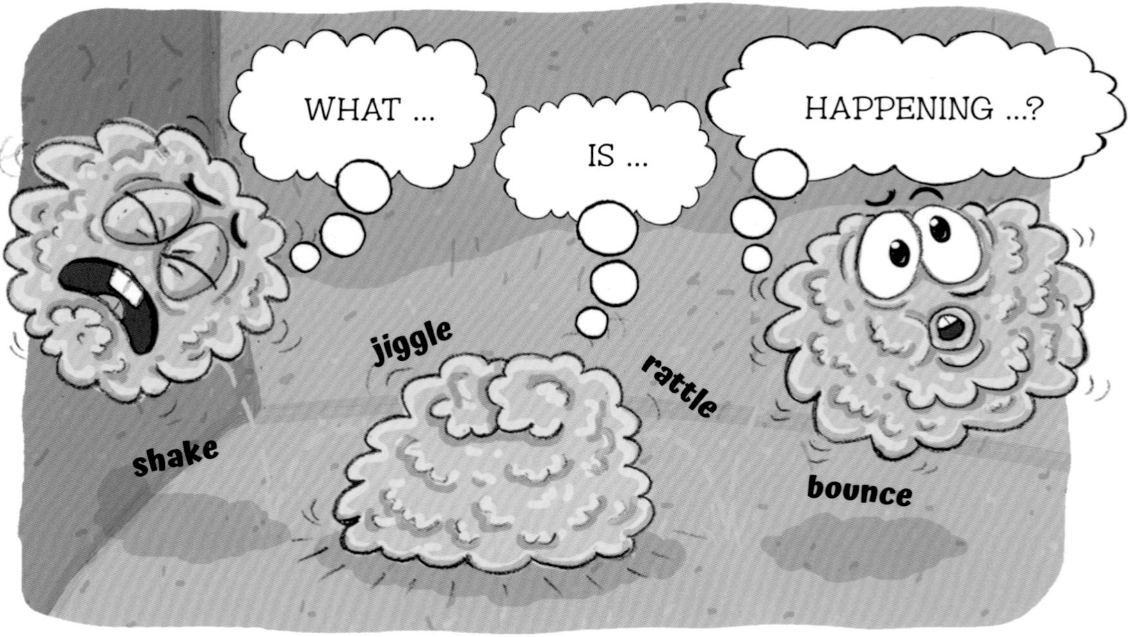
WHAT ...
IS ...
HAPPENING ...?
jiggle
rattle
shake
bounce

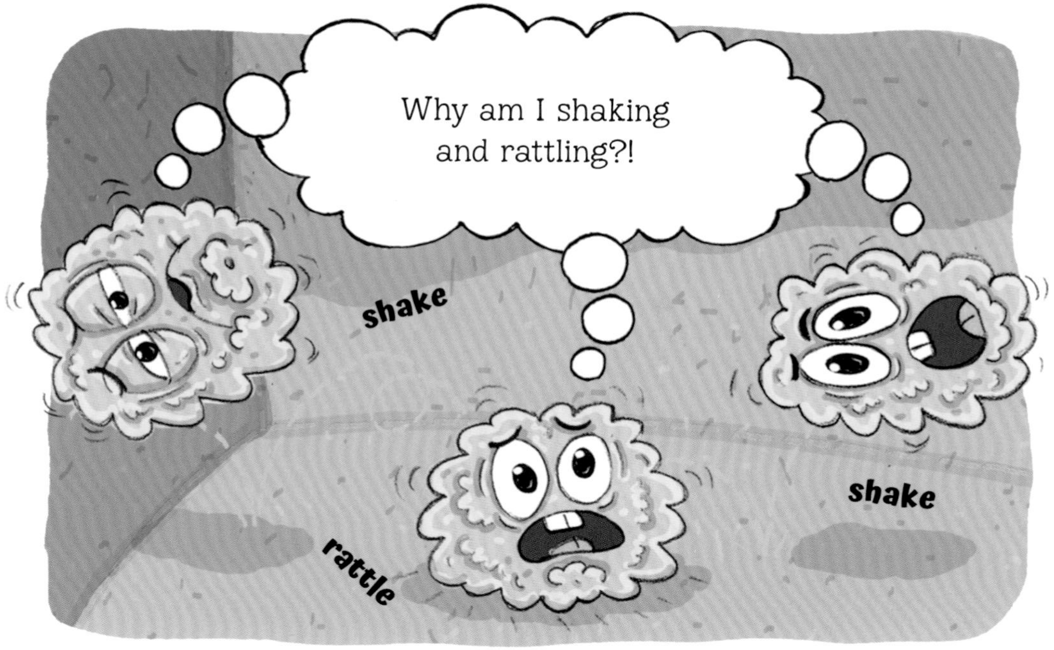

Why am I shaking and rattling?!
shake
rattle
shake

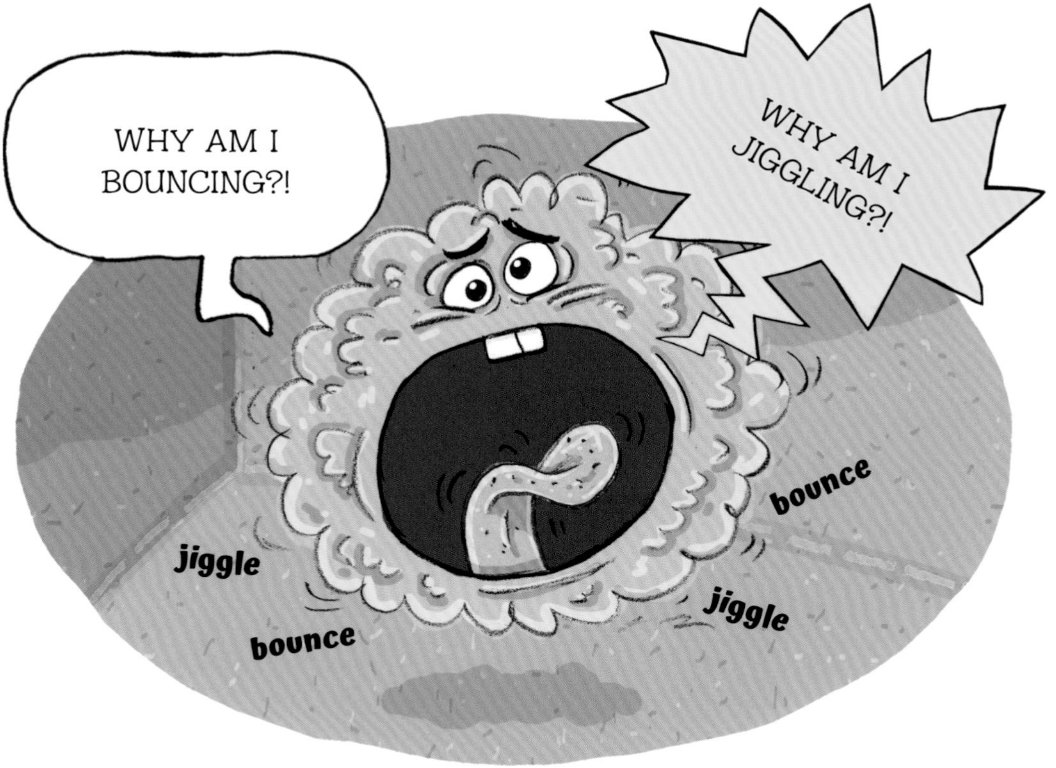

WHY AM I BOUNCING?!
WHY AM I JIGGLING?!
bounce
jiggle
jiggle
bounce

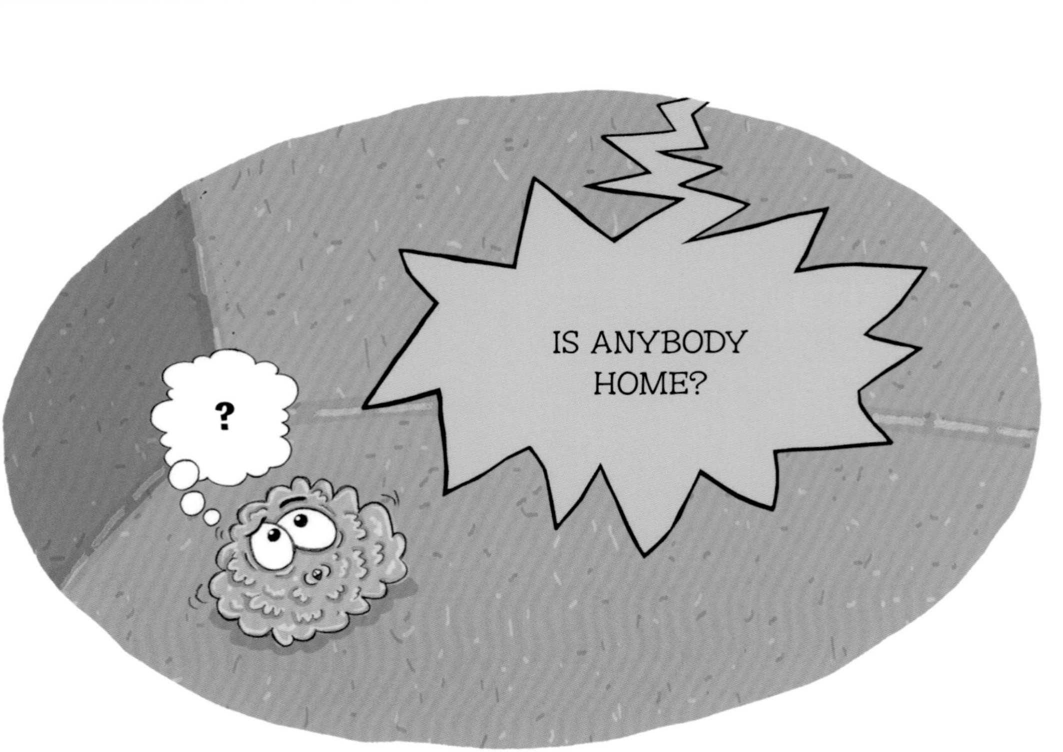
?
IS ANYBODY HOME?

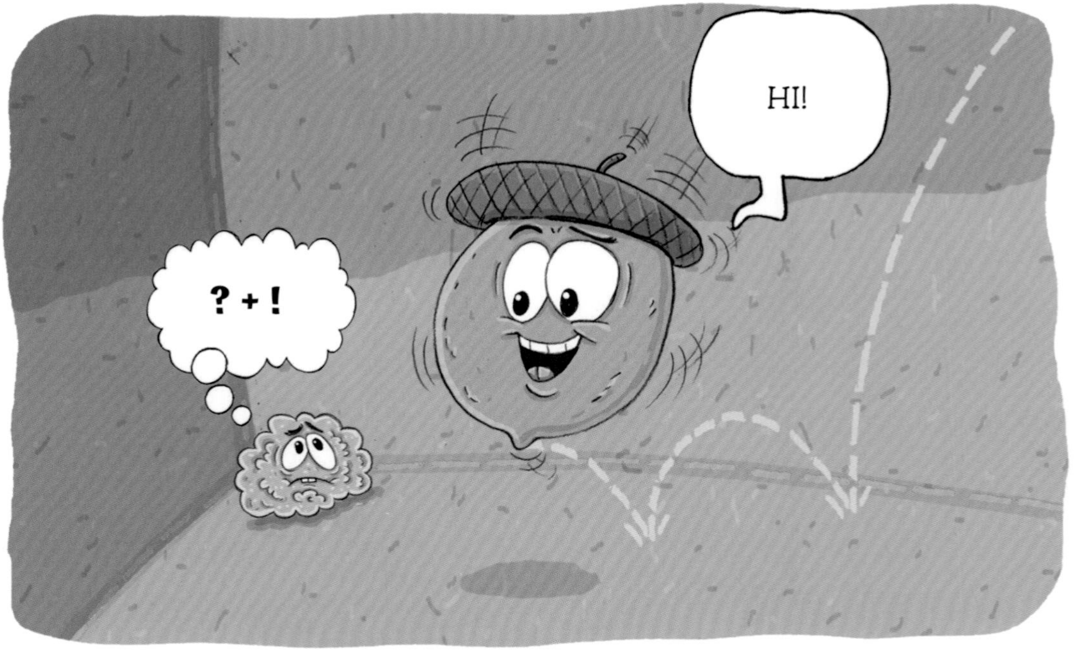
HI!
? + !

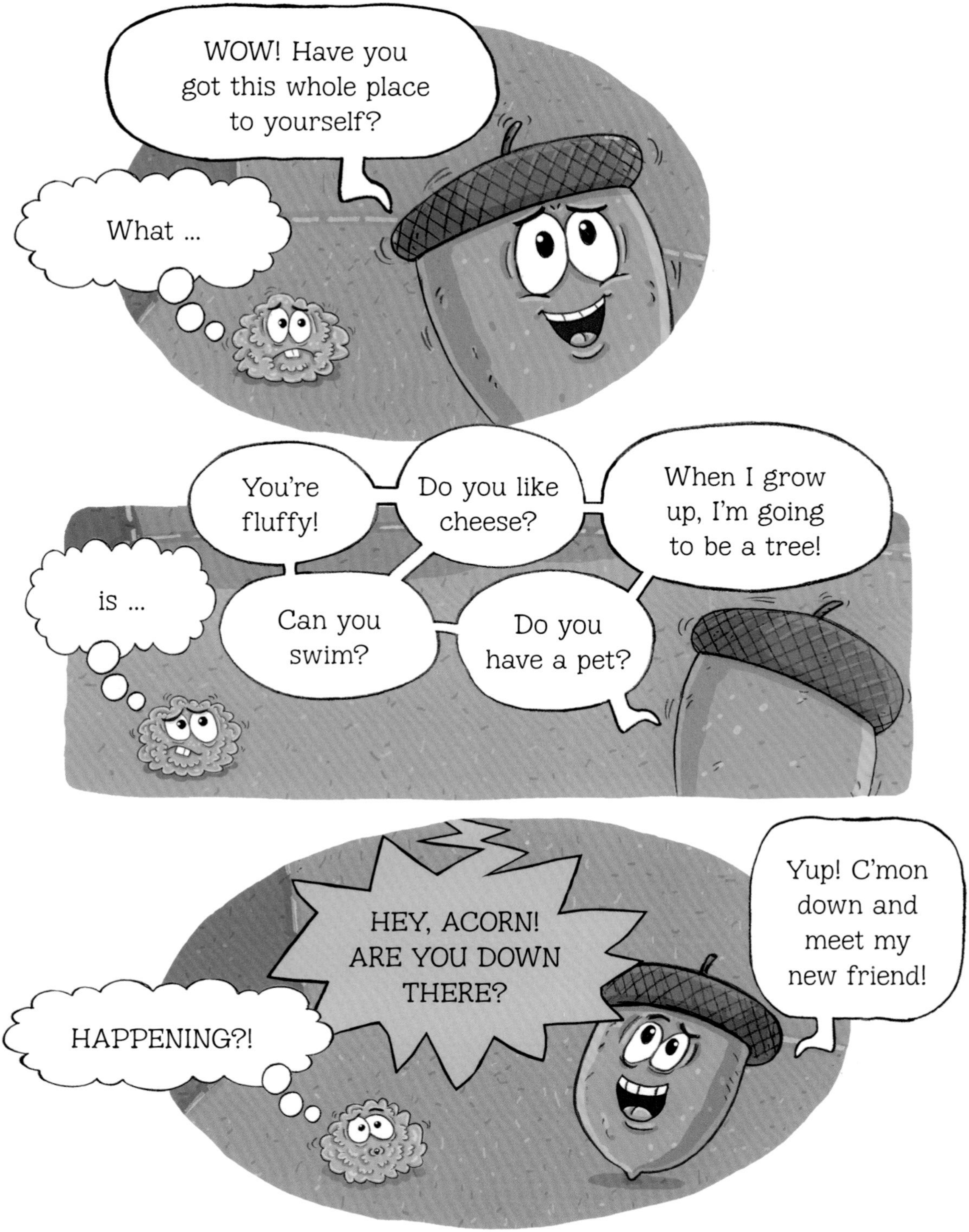
WOW! Have you got this whole place to yourself?
What ...
You're fluffy!
Do you like cheese?
When I grow up, I'm going to be a tree!
is ...
Can you swim?
Do you have a pet?
HEY, ACORN! ARE YOU DOWN THERE?
Yup! C'mon down and meet my new friend!
HAPPENING?!

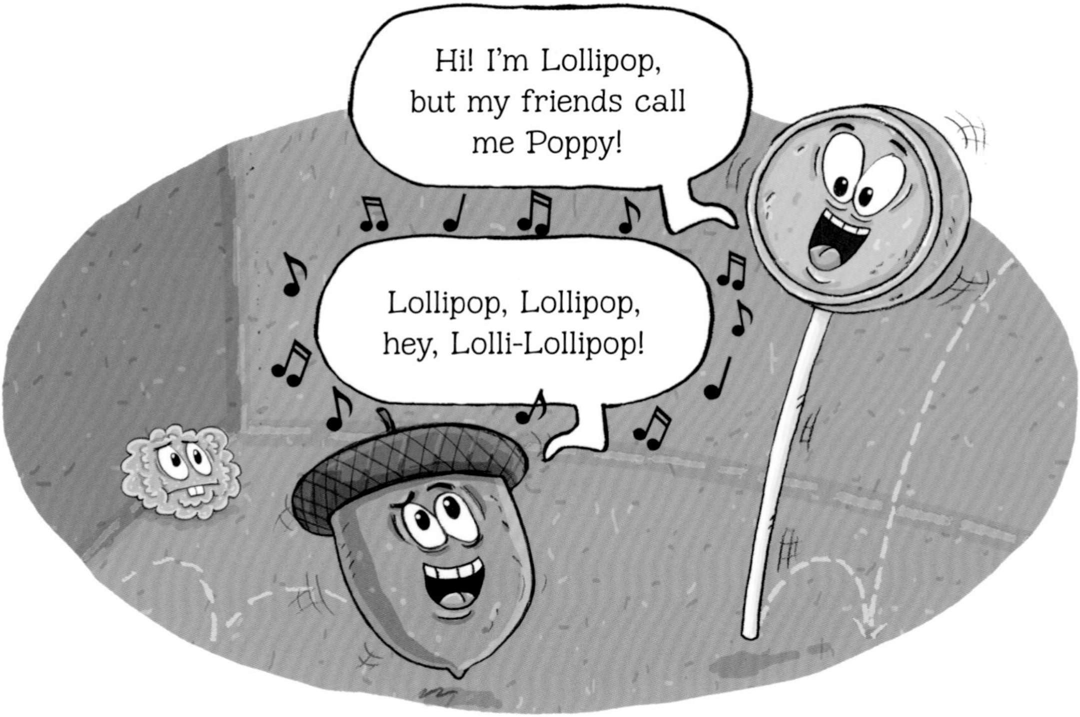
Hi! I'm Lollipop, but my friends call me Poppy!
Lollipop, Lollipop, hey, Lolli-Lollipop!

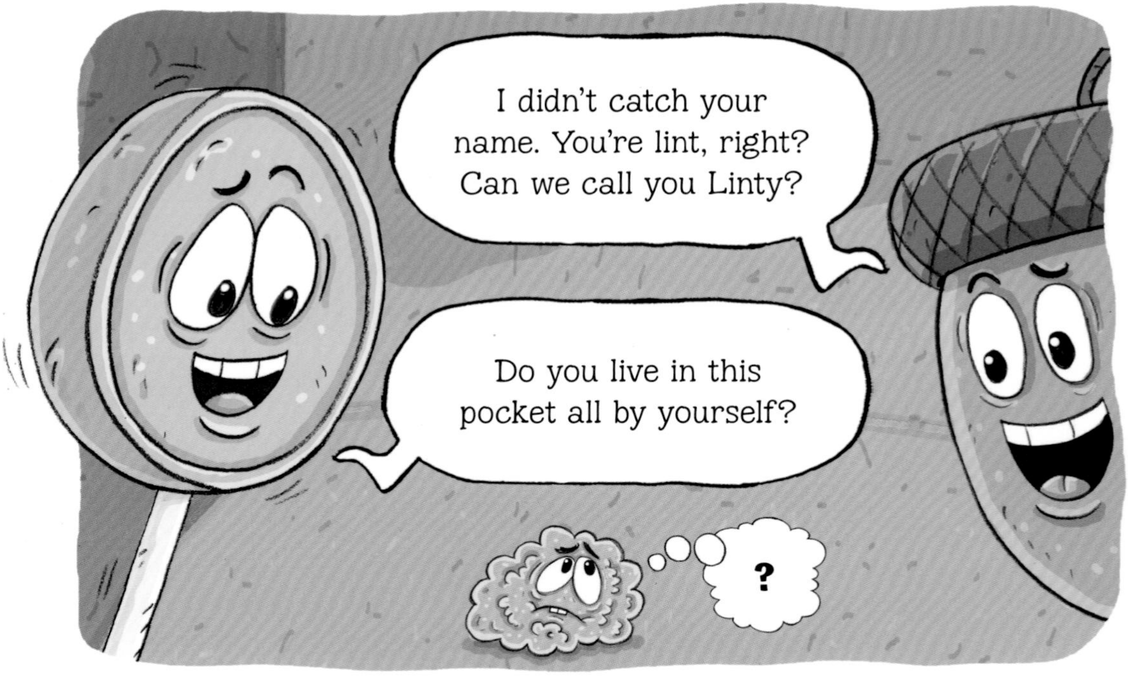
I didn't catch your name. You're lint, right? Can we call you Linty?
Do you live in this pocket all by yourself?
?

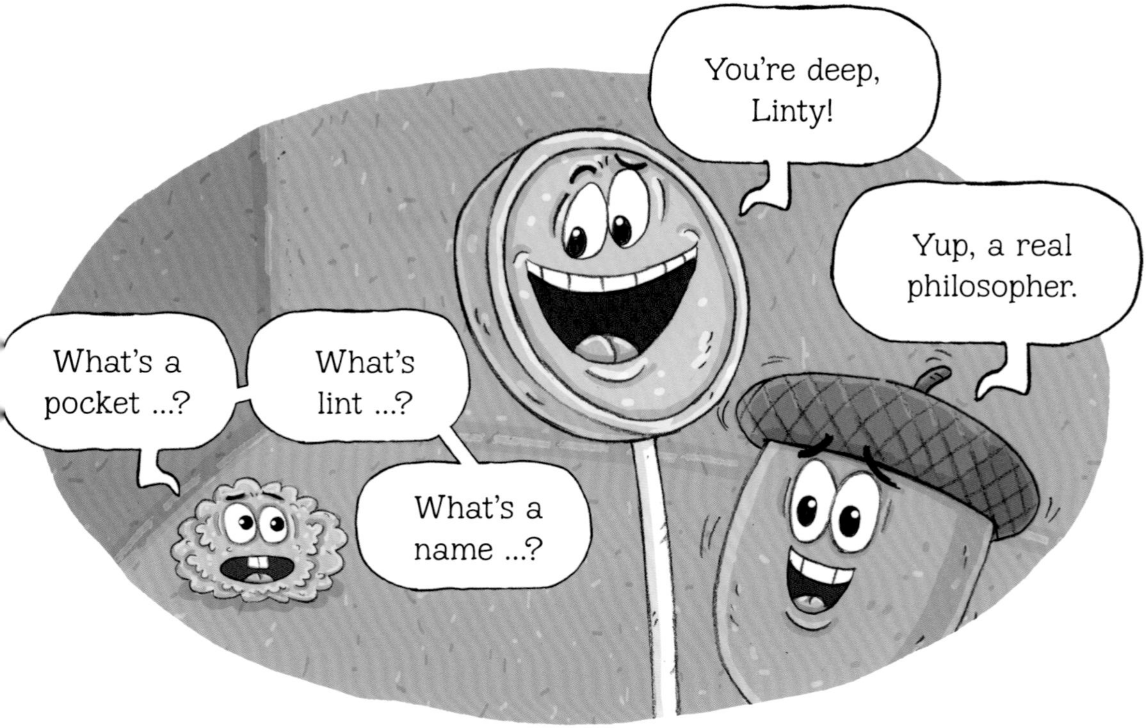
You're deep, Linty!
Yup, a real philosopher.
What's a pocket ...?
What's lint ...?
What's a name ...?

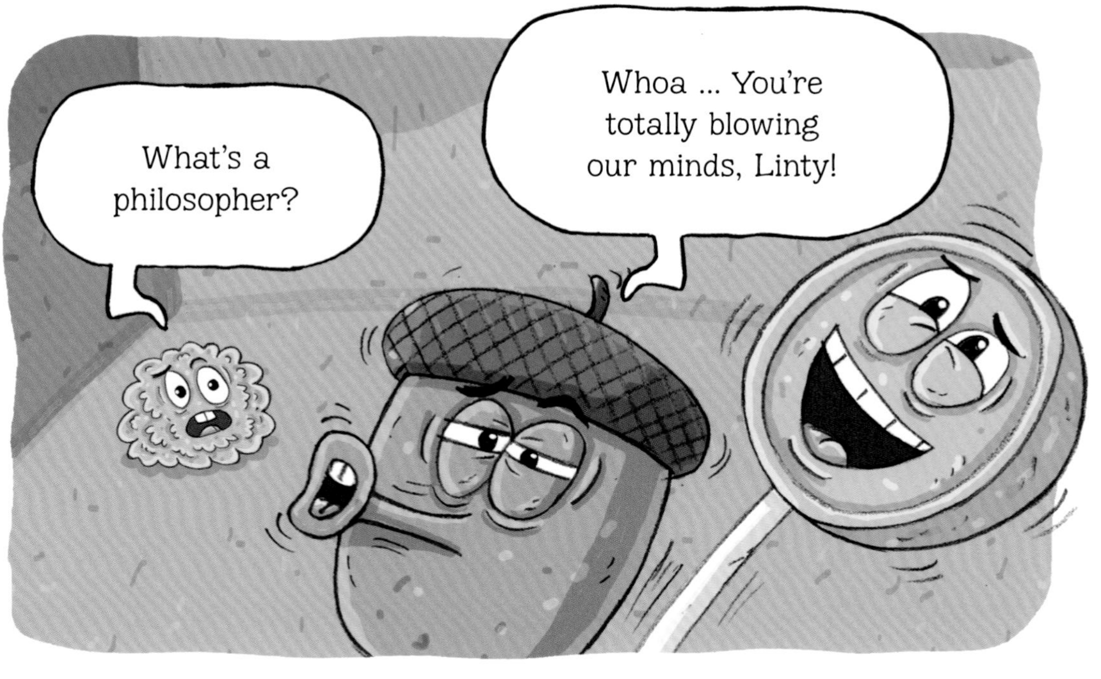
What's a philosopher?
Whoa ... You're totally blowing our minds, Linty!

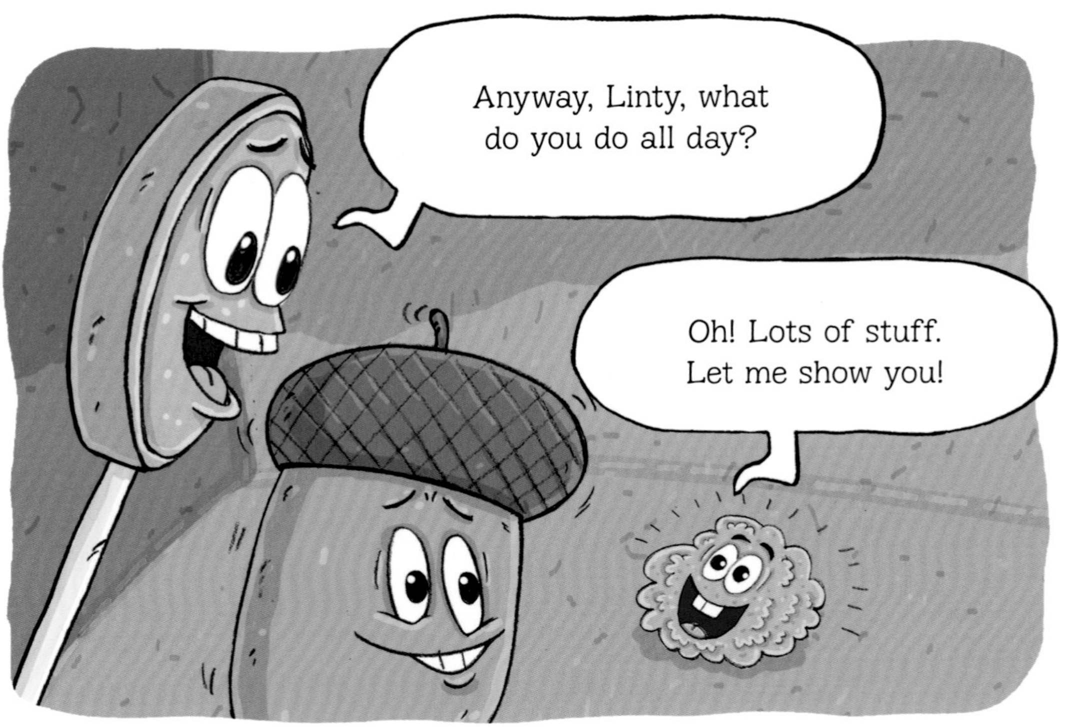
Anyway, Linty, what do you do all day?
Oh! Lots of stuff. Let me show you!

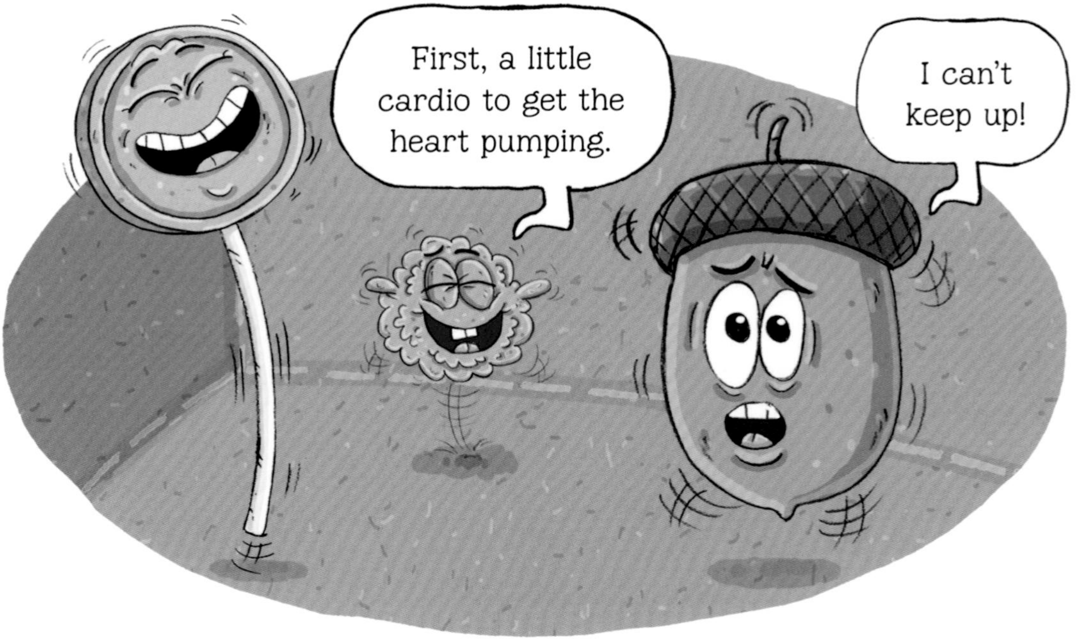
First, a little cardio to get the heart pumping.
I can't keep up!

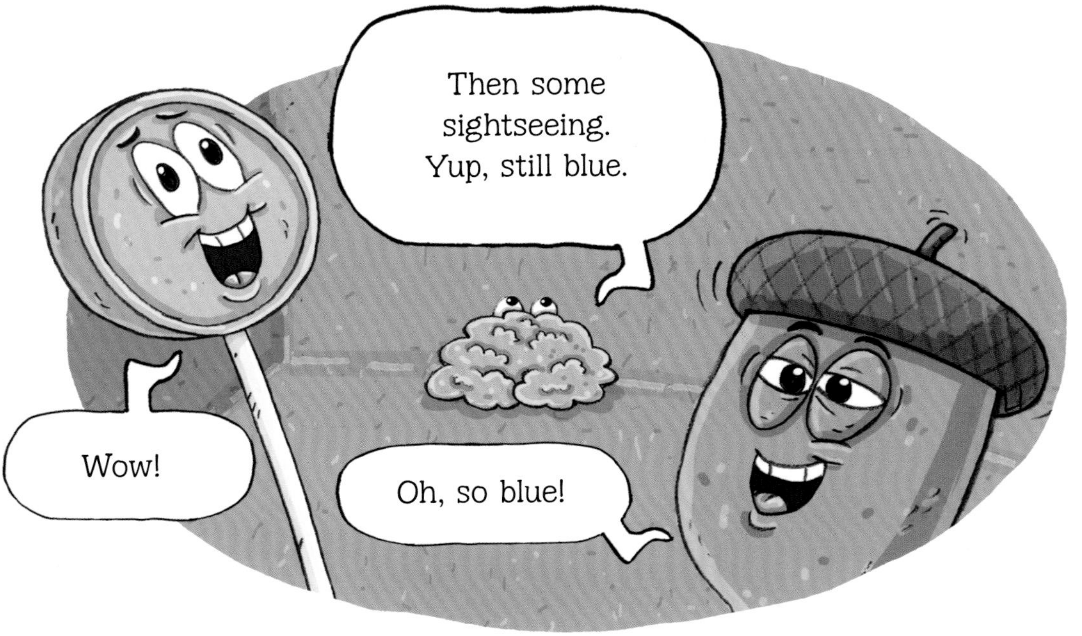
Then some sightseeing. Yup, still blue.
Wow!
Oh, so blue!

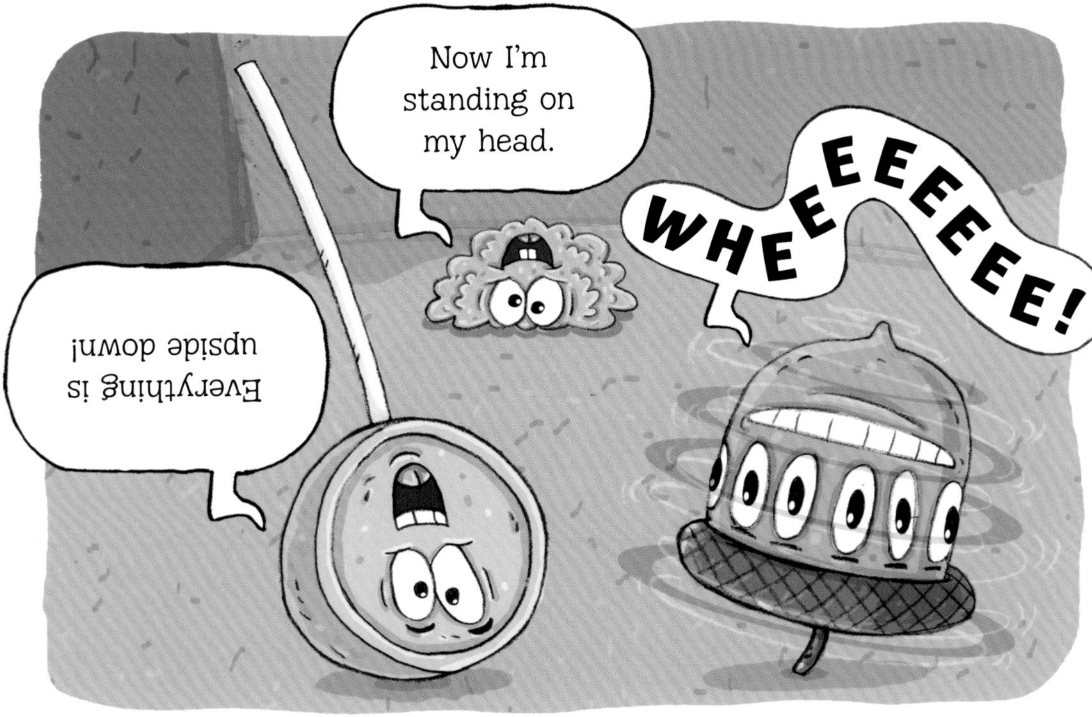
Now I'm standing on my head.
Everything is upside down!
WHEEEEEEEE!

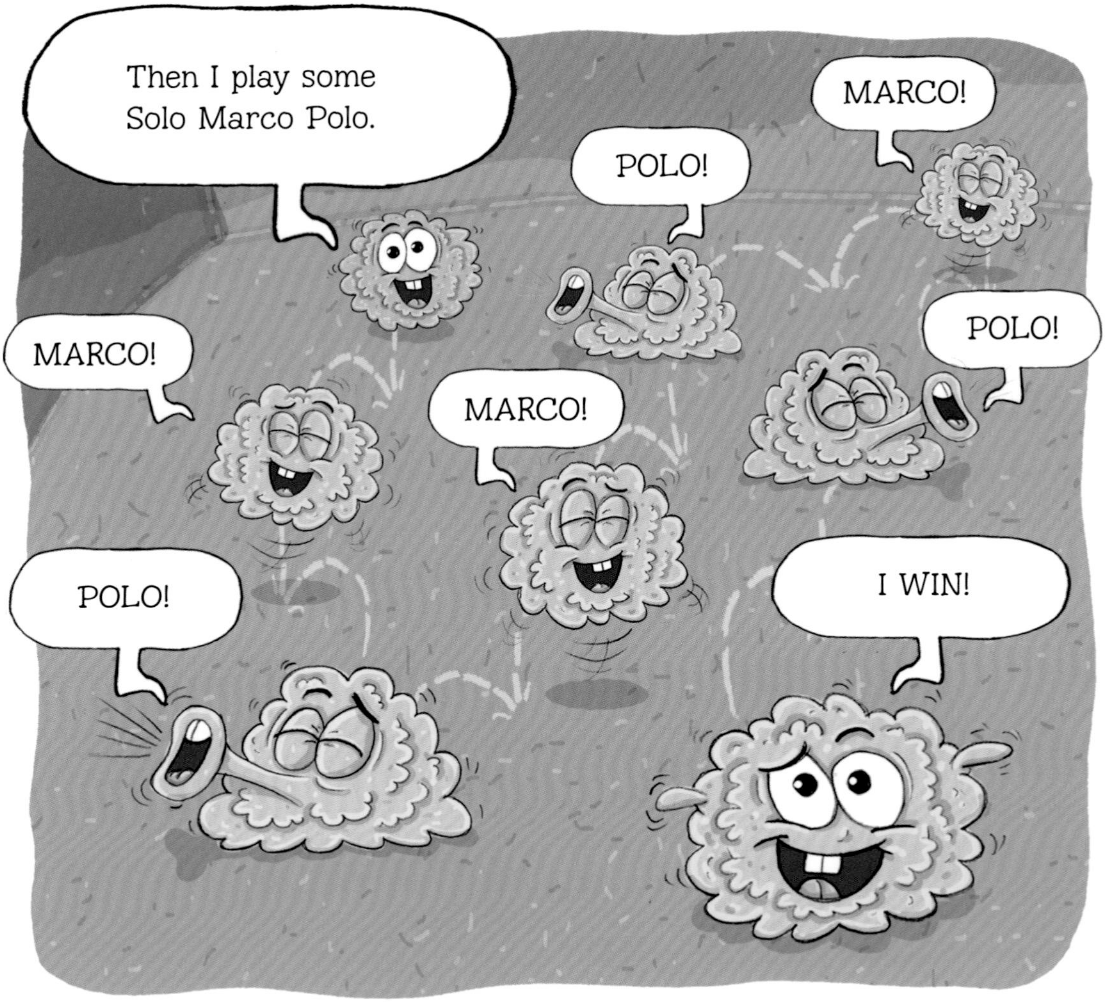
Then I play some Solo Marco Polo.
MARCO!
POLO!
MARCO!
POLO!
MARCO!
POLO!
I WIN!

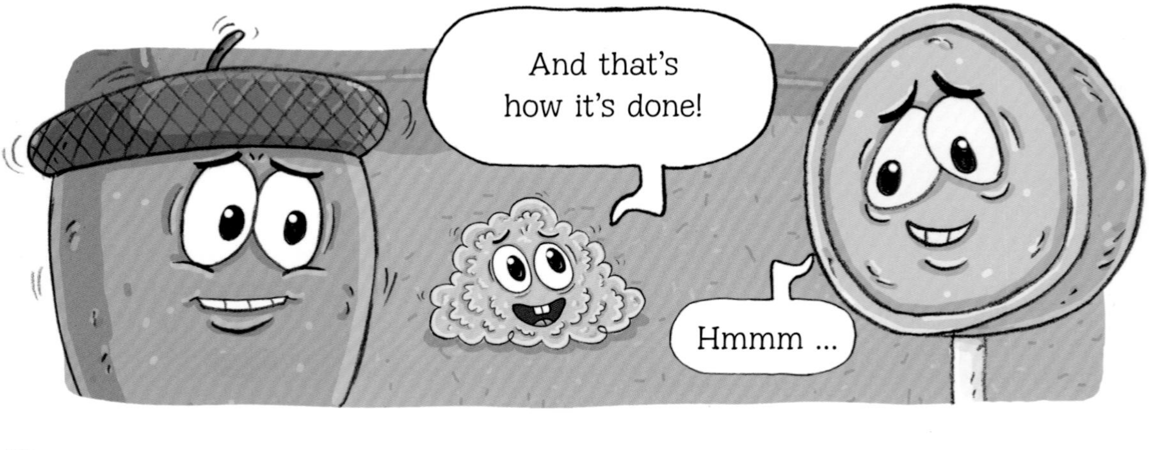
And that's how it's done!
Hmmm ...

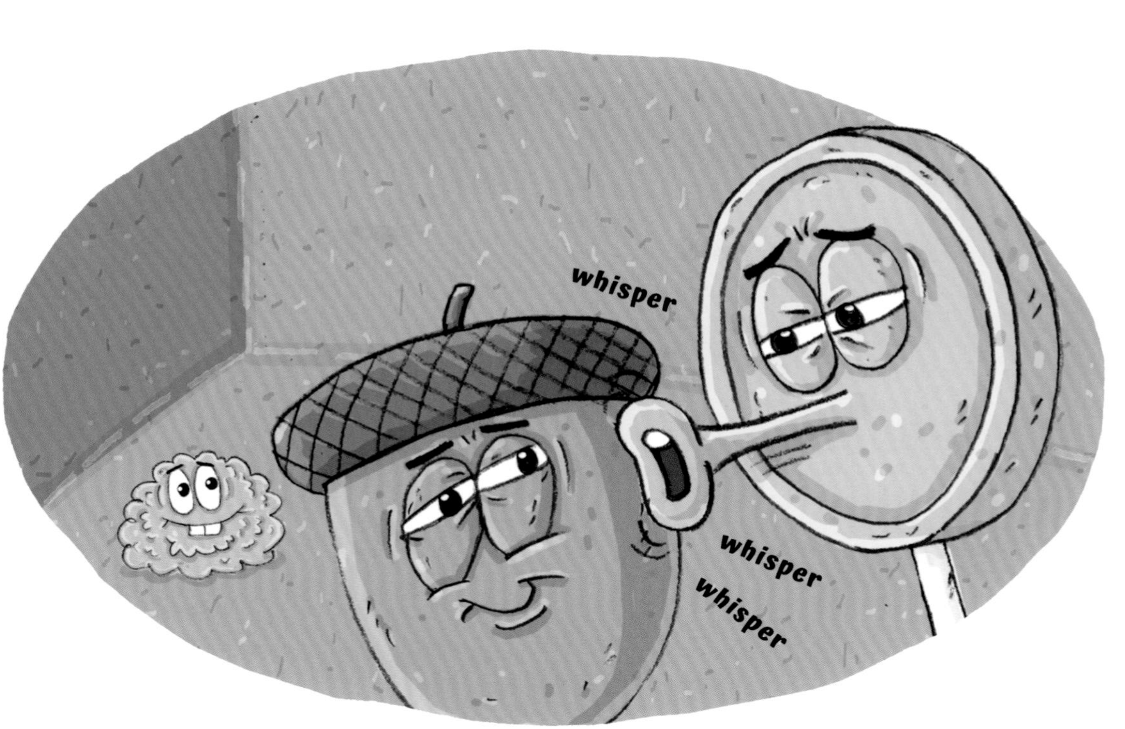
whisper
whisper
whisper

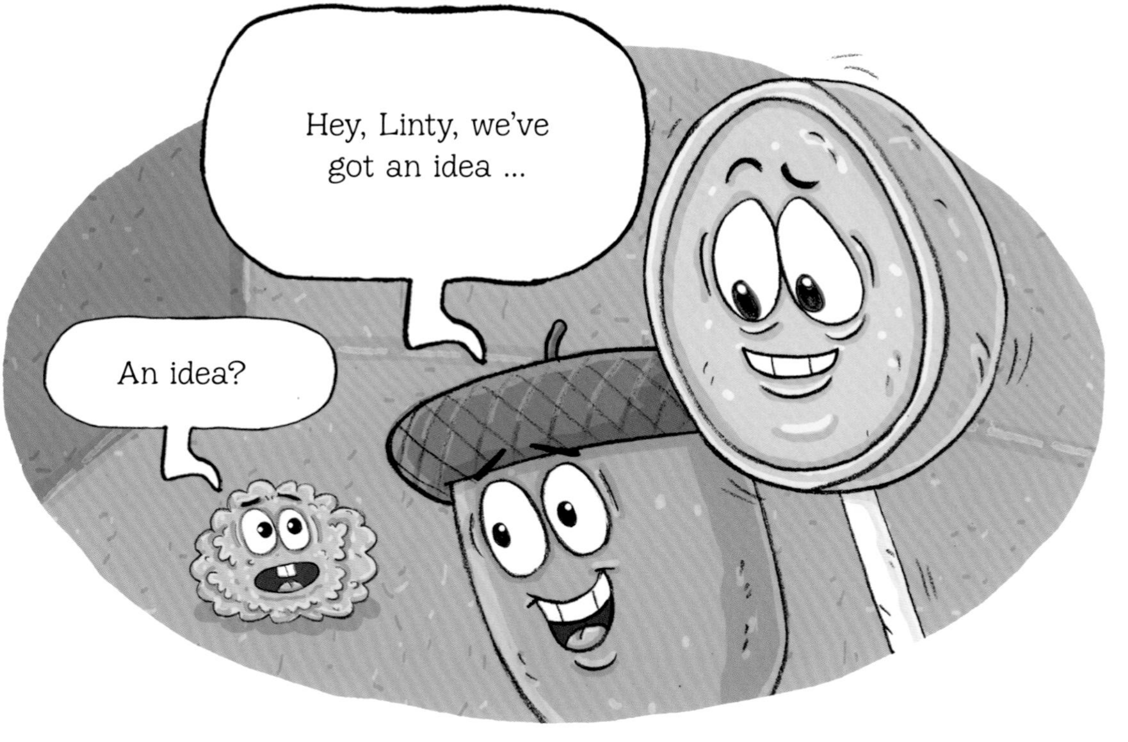
Hey, Linty, we've got an idea ...
An idea?

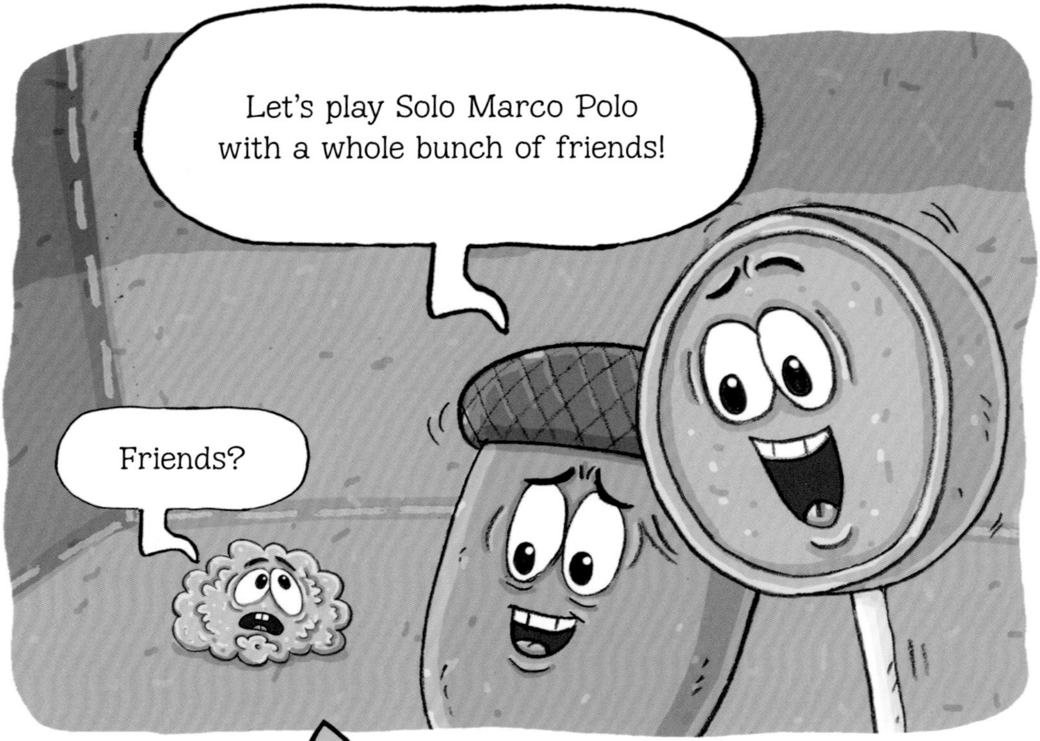
Let's play Solo Marco Polo with a whole bunch of friends!
Friends?

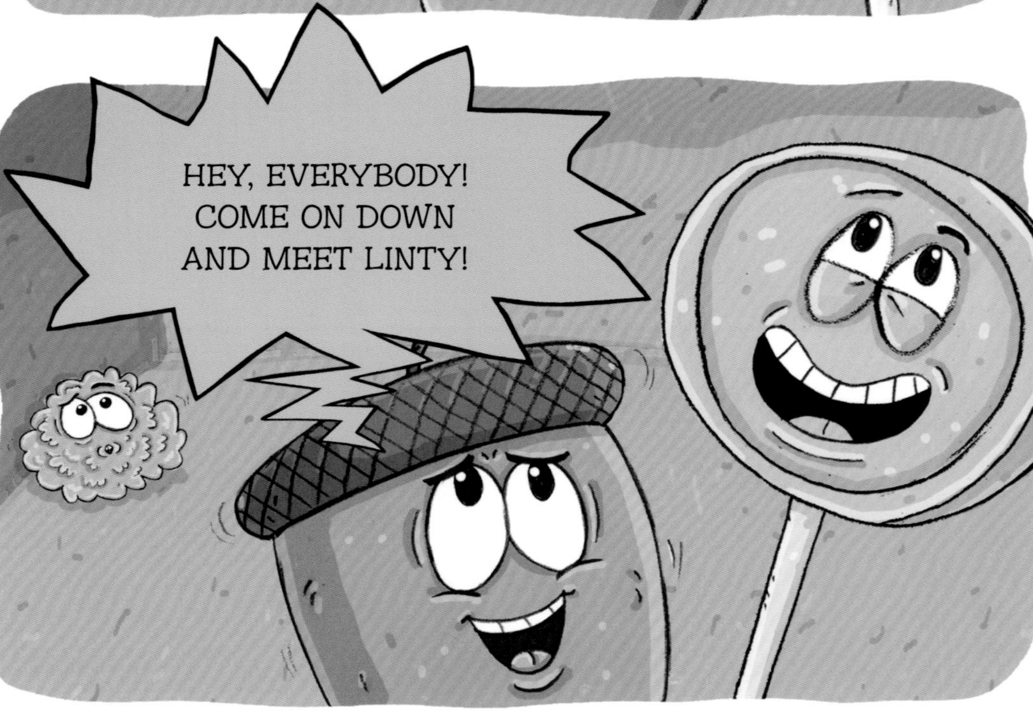
HEY, EVERYBODY! COME ON DOWN AND MEET LINTY!

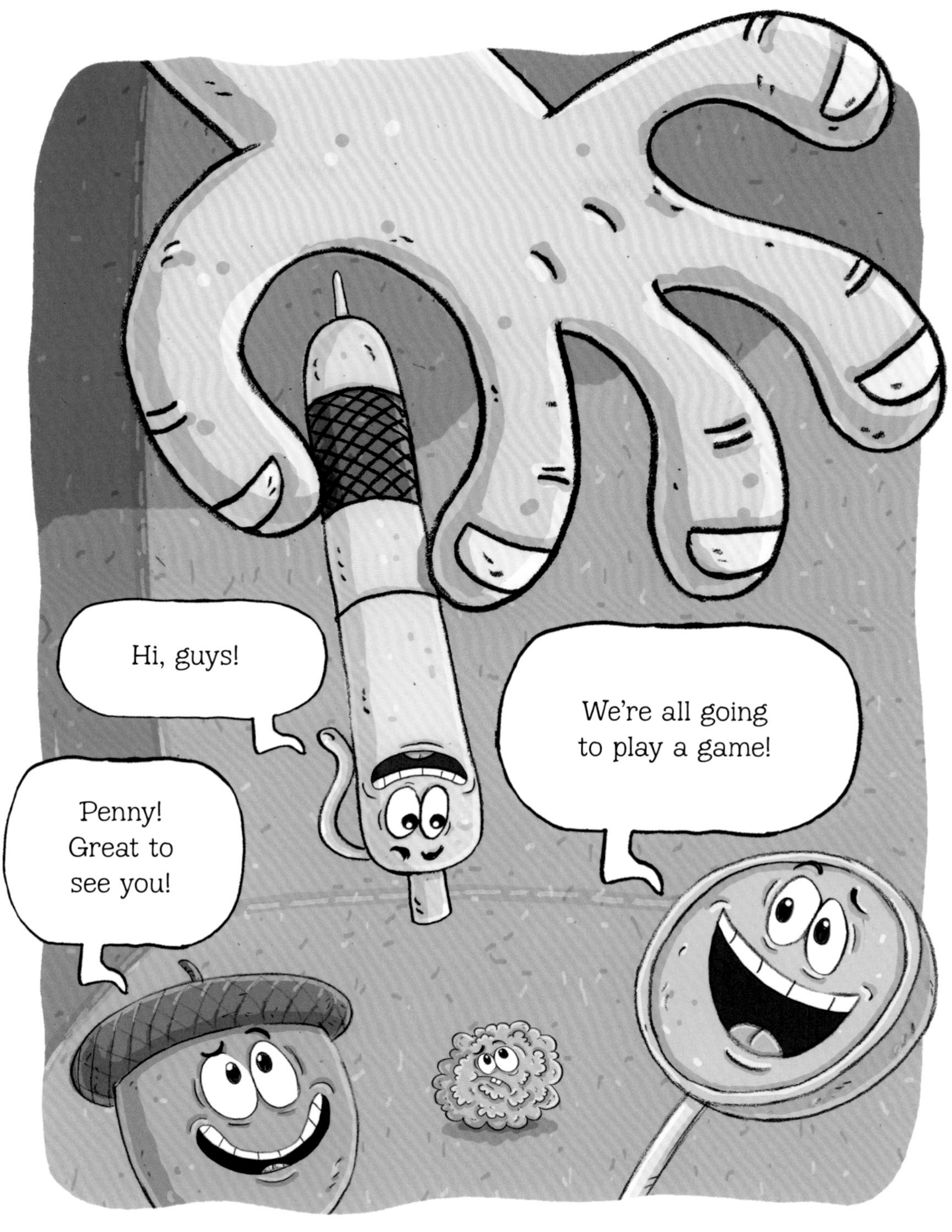
Hi, guys!
We're all going to play a game!
Penny! Great to see you!

MORE AND MORE GUESTS DROPPED IN.

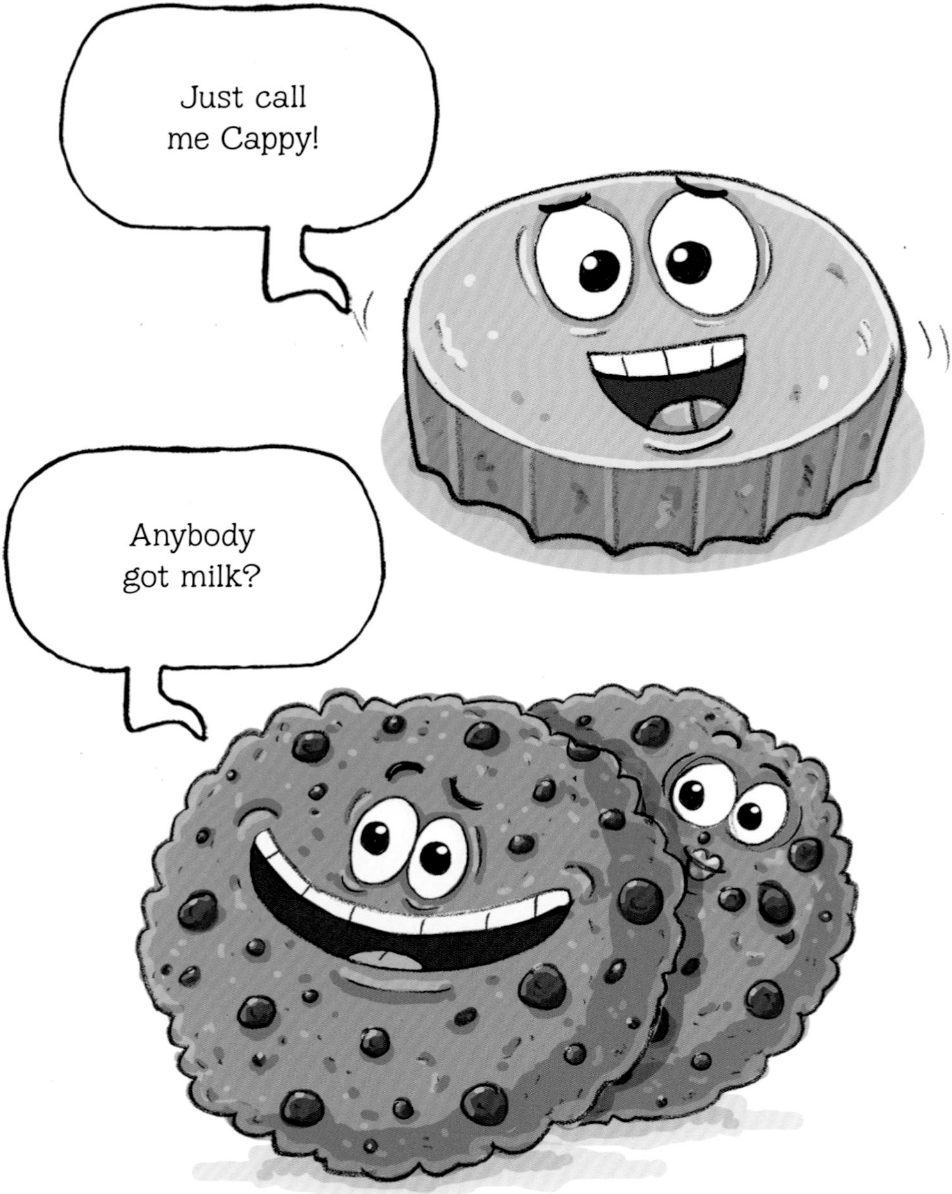
Just call me Cappy!
Anybody got milk?

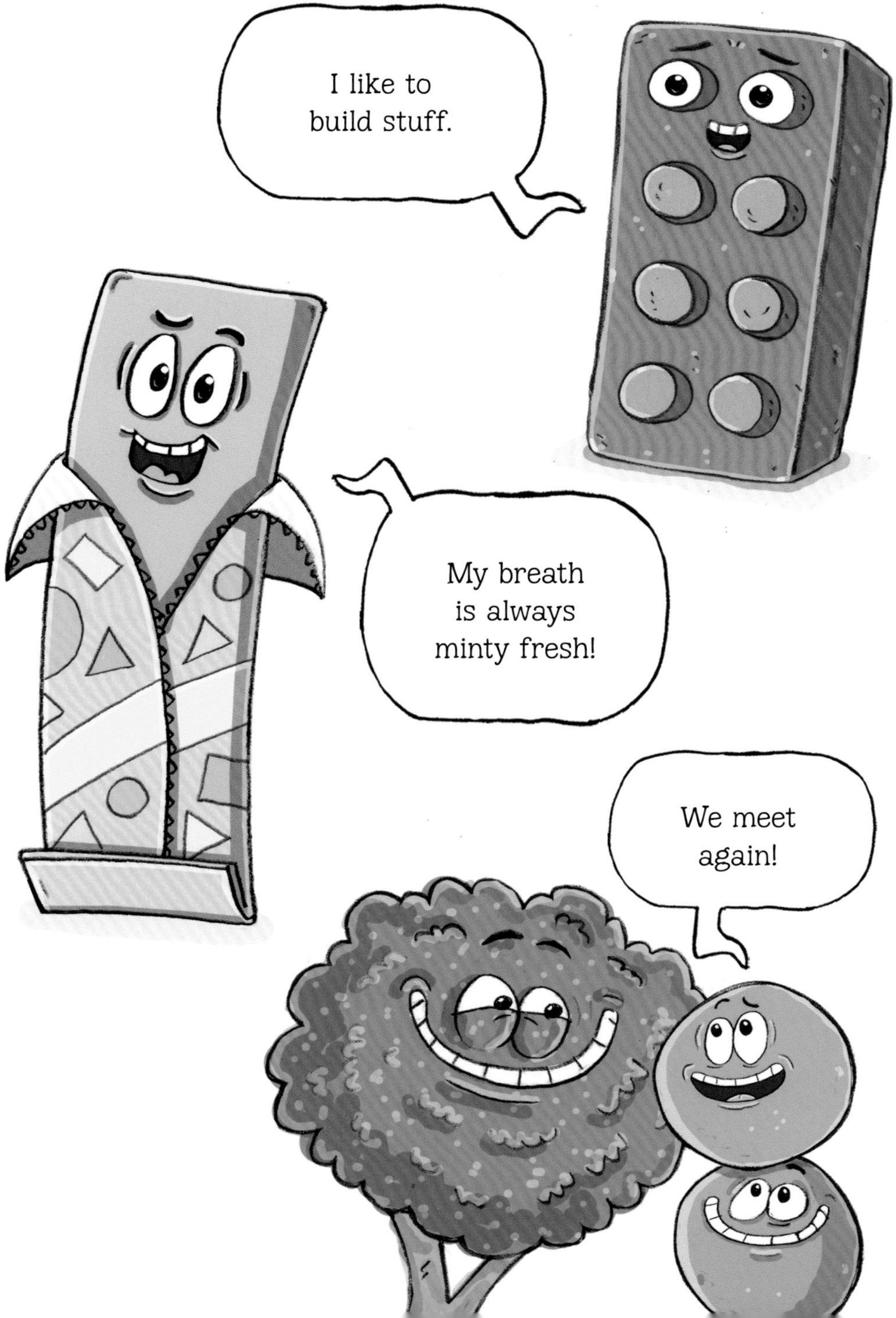
I like to build stuff.
My breath is always minty fresh!
We meet again!

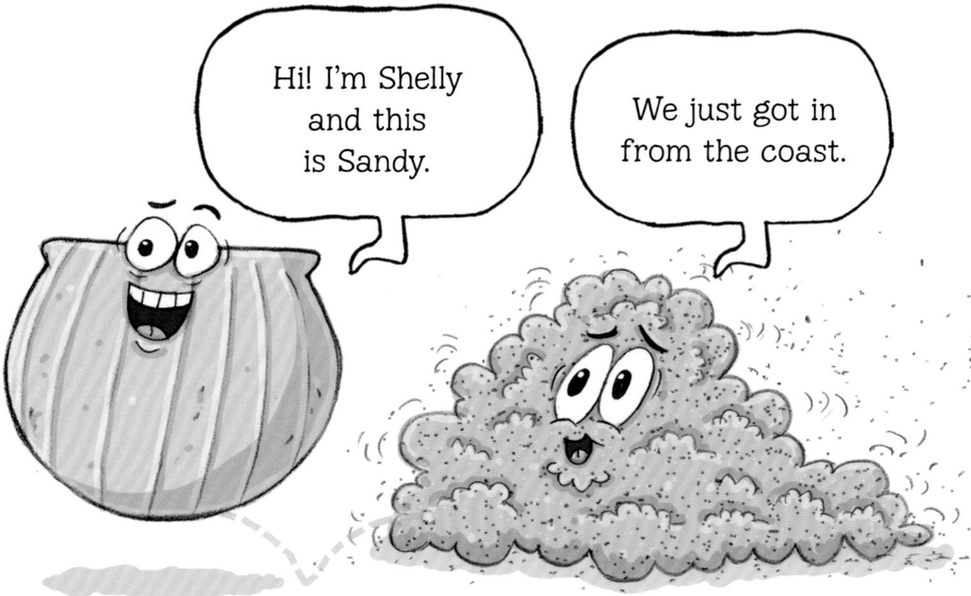
Hi! I'm Shelly and this is Sandy.
We just got in from the coast.

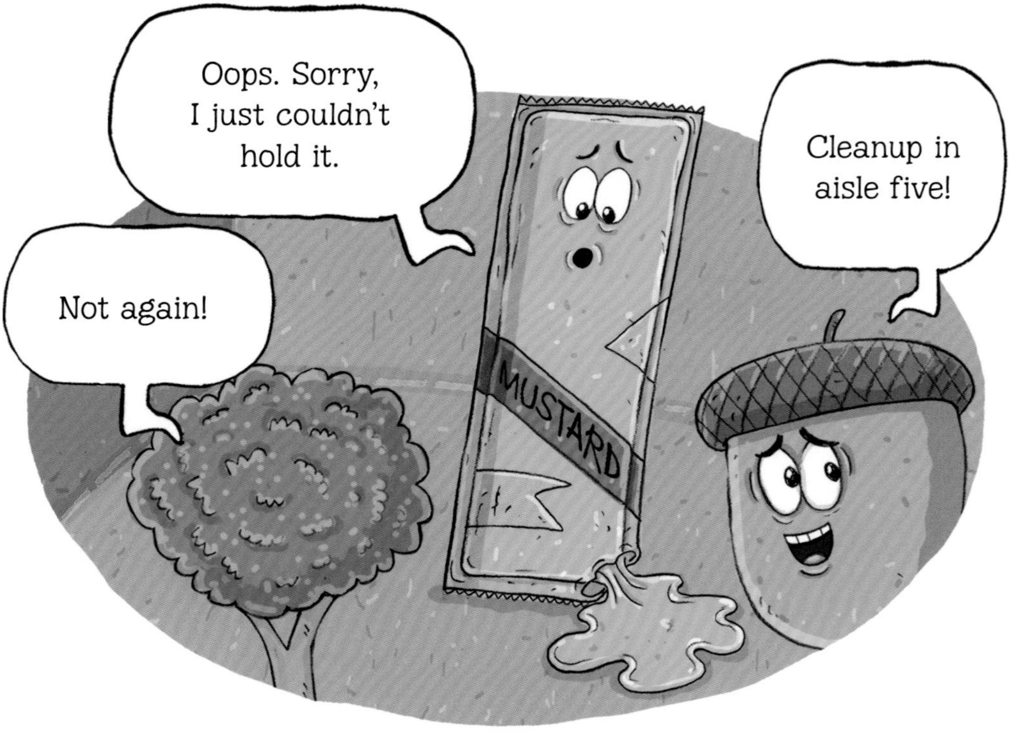
Oops. Sorry, I just couldn't hold it.
Not again!
MUSTARD
Cleanup in aisle five!

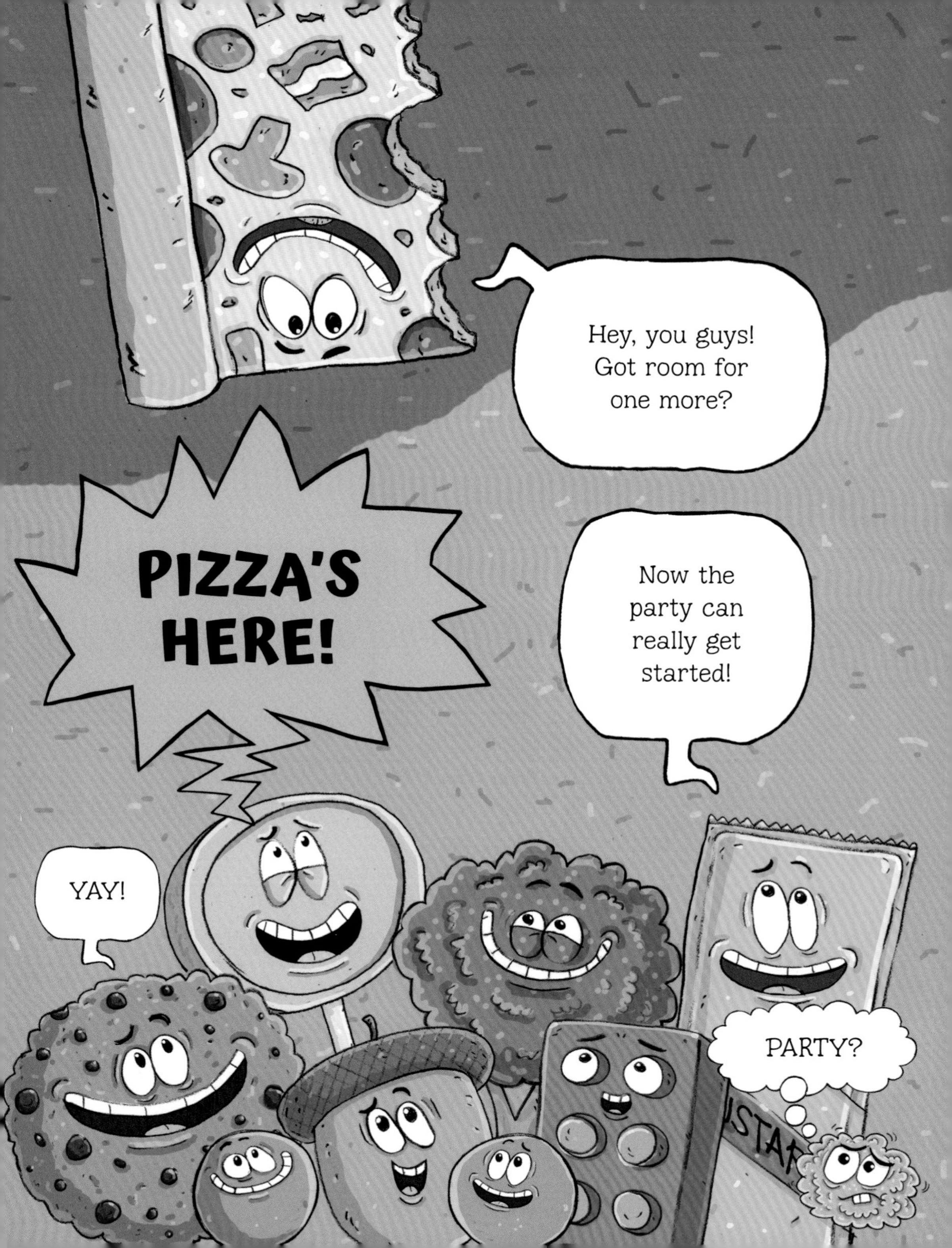
Hey, you guys! Got room for one more?
PIZZA'S HERE!
Now the party can really get started!
YAY!
PARTY?

SO LINTY TRIED OUT A NEW WAY

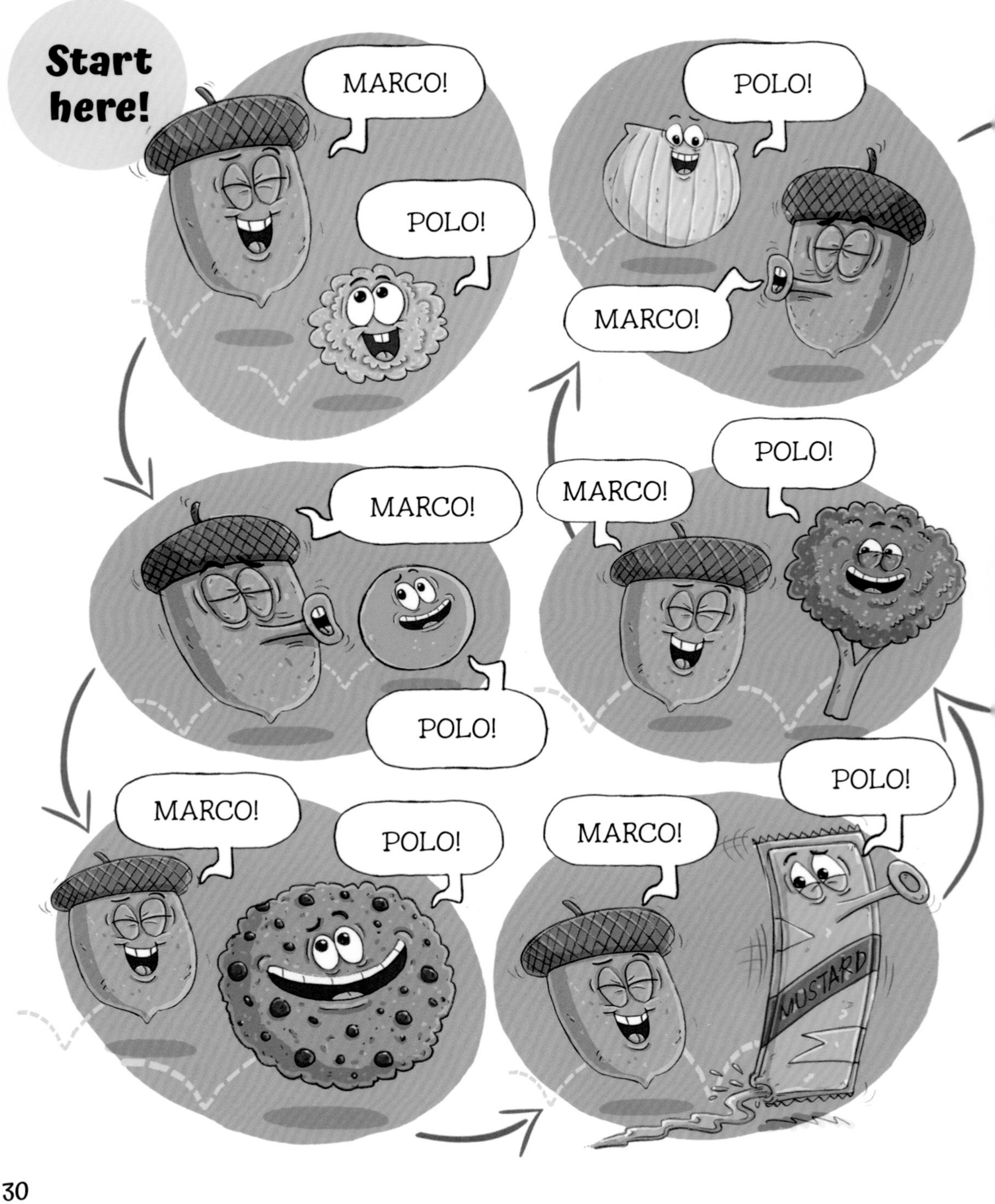
Start here!
MARCO!
POLO!
MARCO!
POLO!
MARCO!
POLO!
MARCO!
POLO!
MUSTARD
MARCO!
POLO!
POLO!
MARCO!

OF PLAYING SOLO MARCO POLO.

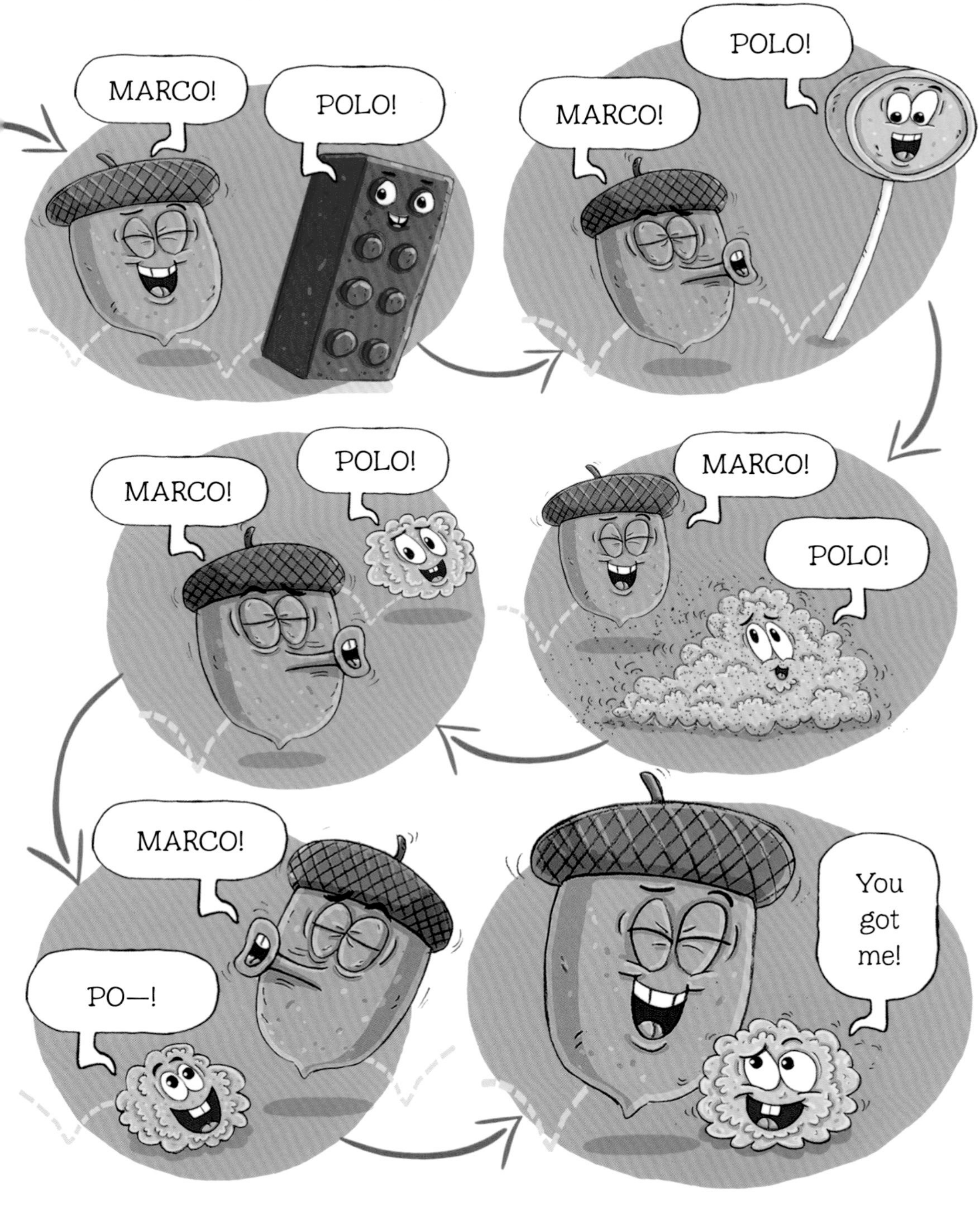
MARCO!
POLO!
MARCO!
POLO!
MARCO!
POLO!
MARCO!
POLO!
MARCO!
PO—!
You got me!

THEN THINGS GOT PRETTY WILD.

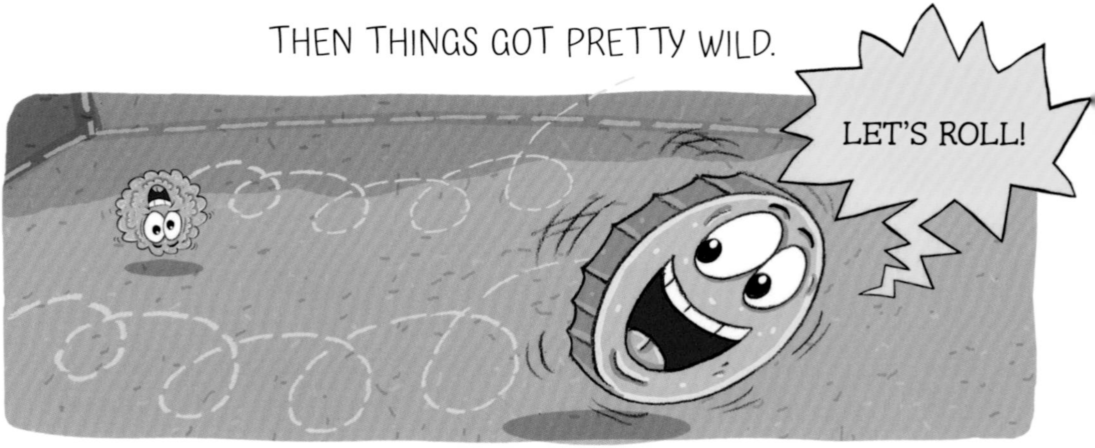
LET'S ROLL!

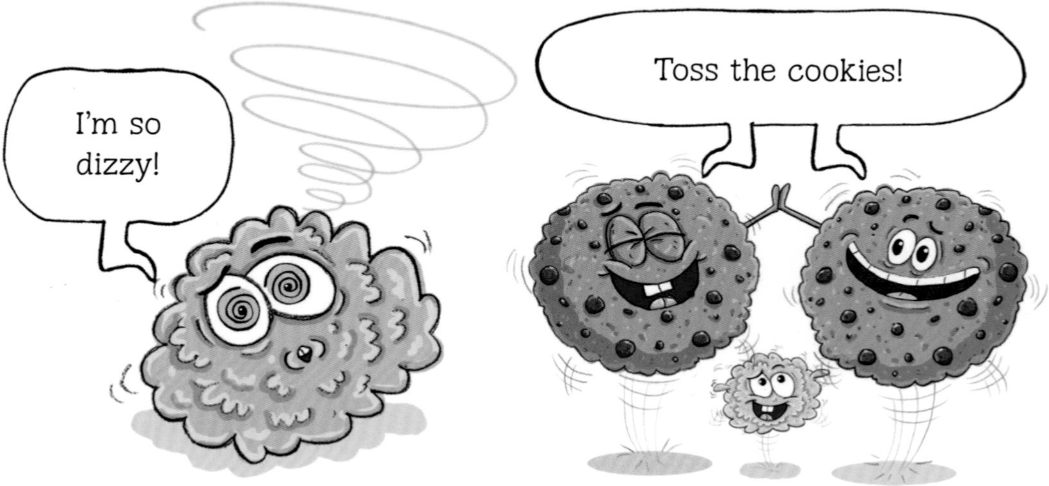
I'm so dizzy!
Toss the cookies!

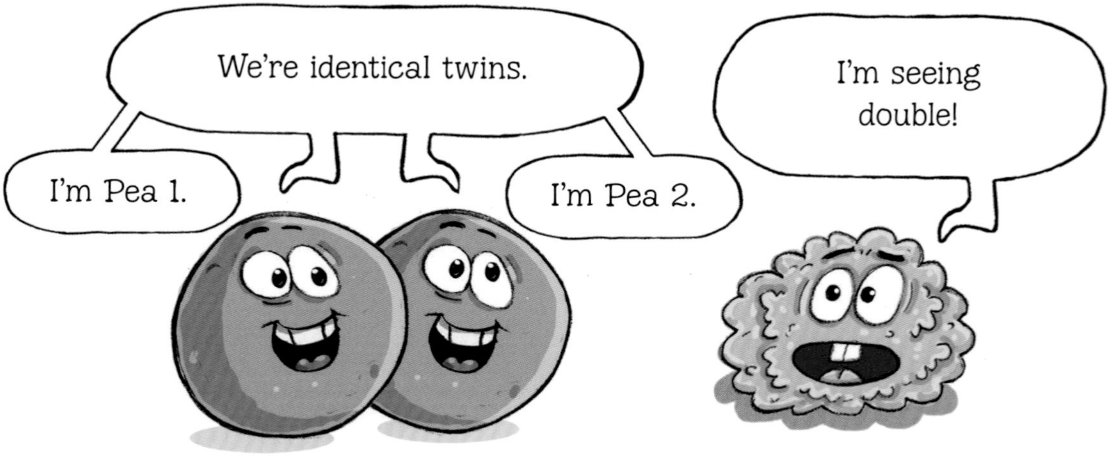
We're identical twins.
I'm Pea 1.
I'm Pea 2.
I'm seeing double!

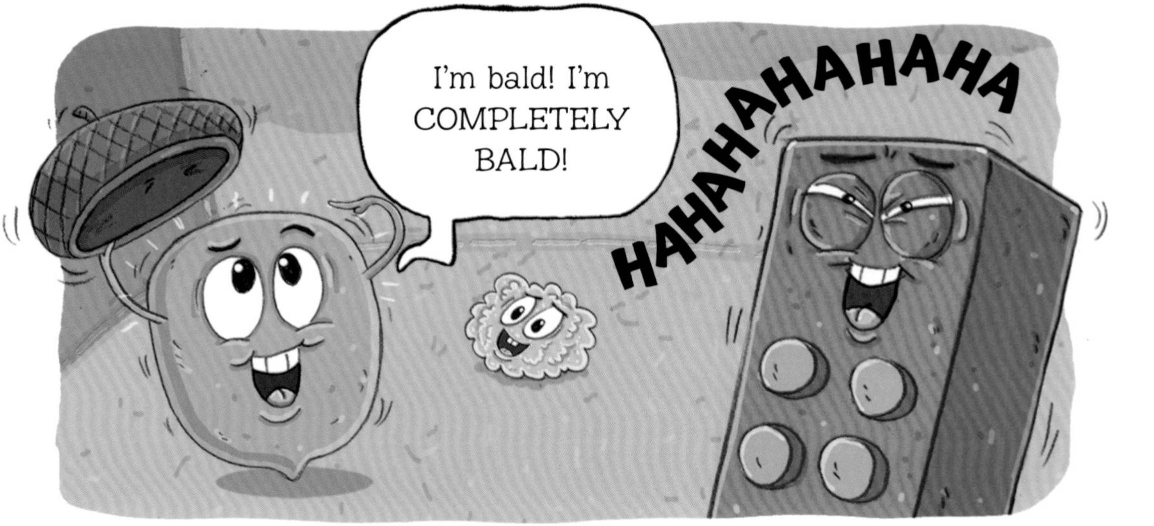
I'm bald! I'm COMPLETELY BALD!
HAHAHAHAHAHAHA

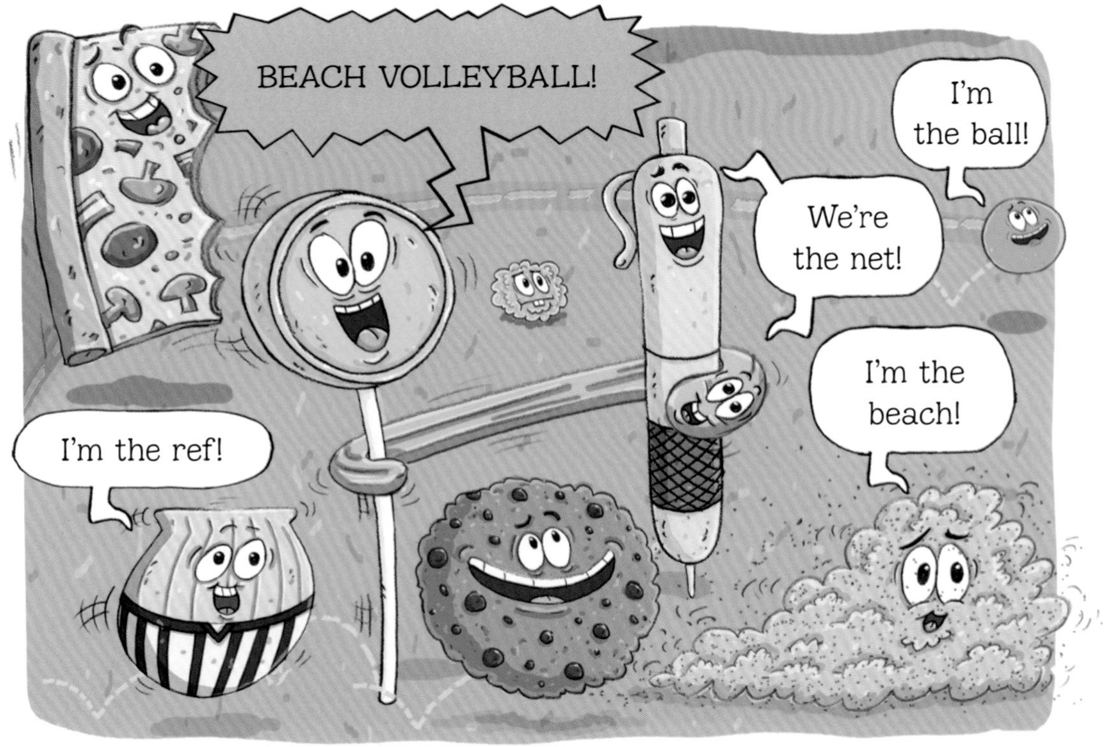
BEACH VOLLEYBALL!
I'm the ball!
We're the net!
I'm the beach!
I'm the ref!

LINTY HAD NEVER SEEN SO MANY AMAZING SIGHTS, HEARD SO MANY SOUNDS OR SMELLED SO MANY SMELLS!

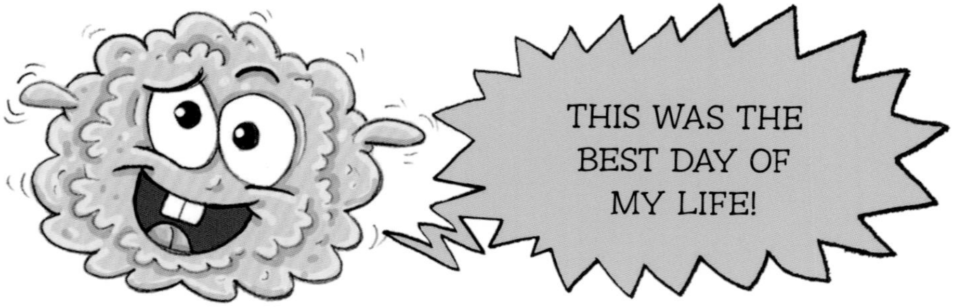
THIS WAS THE BEST DAY OF MY LIFE!

BUT LET'S FACE IT. UP TO THIS POINT, LINTY HAD LIVED A PRETTY SHELTERED LIFE.

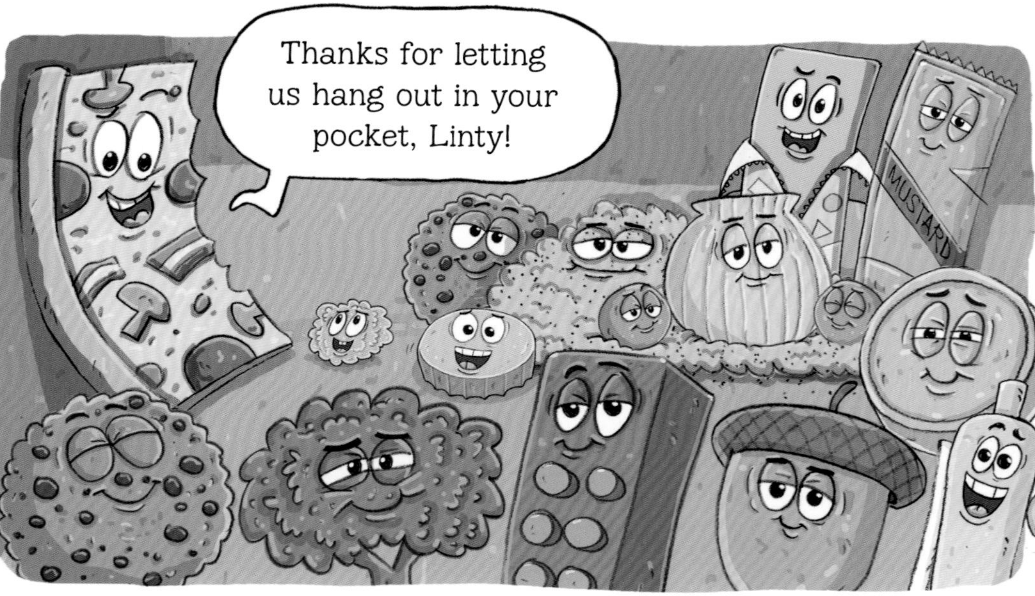
Thanks for letting us hang out in your pocket, Linty!
MUSTARD

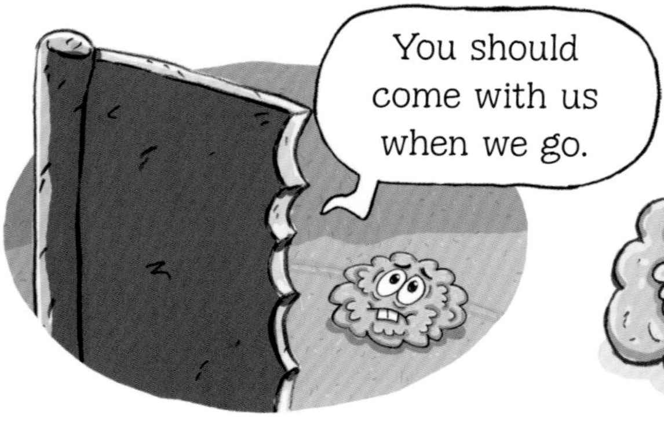
You should come with us when we go.

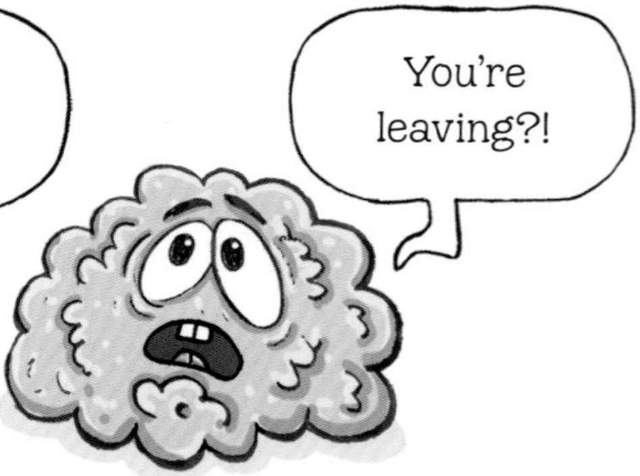
You're leaving?!

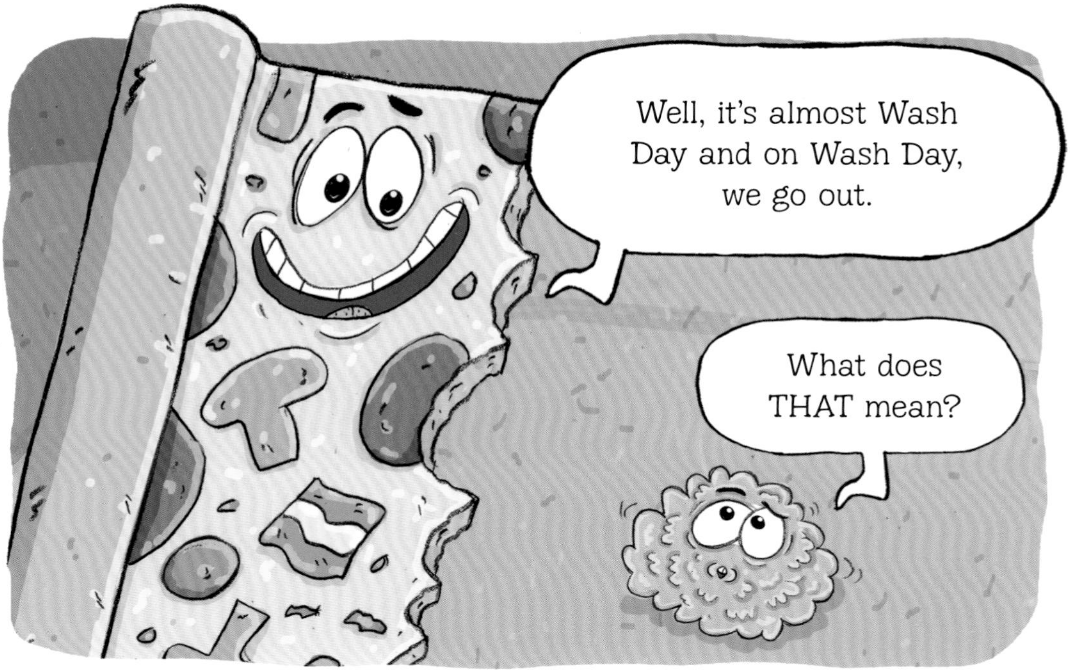
Well, it's almost Wash Day and on Wash Day, we go out.
What does THAT mean?

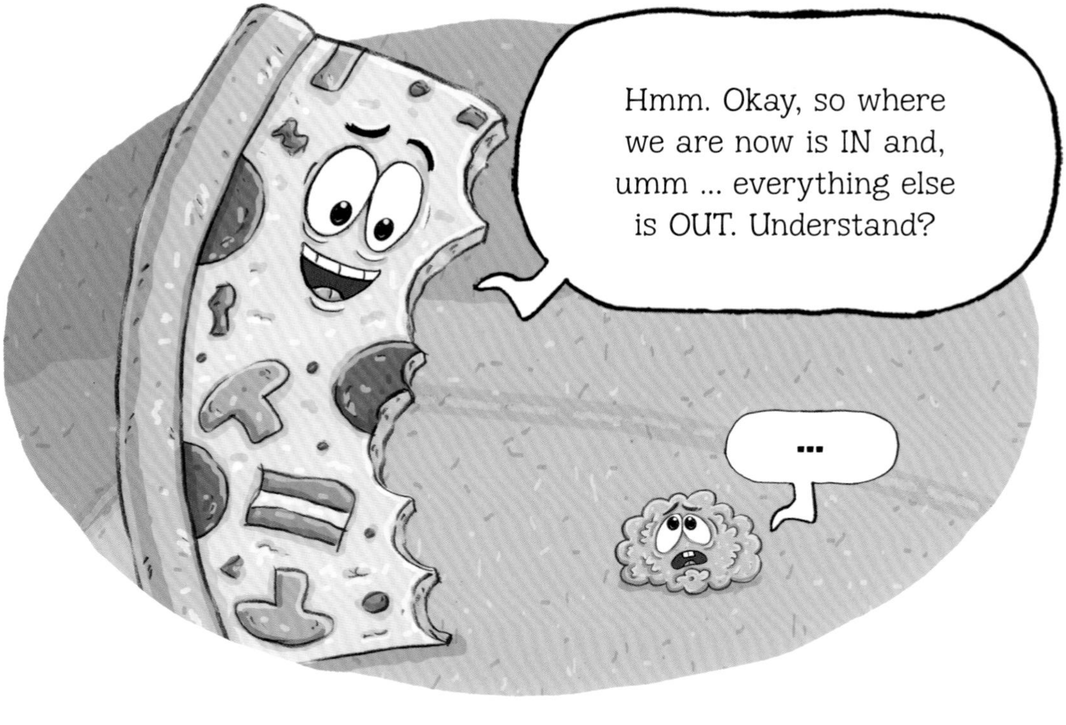
Hmm. Okay, so where we are now is IN and, umm ... everything else is OUT. Understand?
...

BEFORE LINTY COULD ASK ANY MORE QUESTIONS, SOMEONE YELLED ...

WASH DAY!

REMEMBER TO EMPTY YOUR POCKETS!

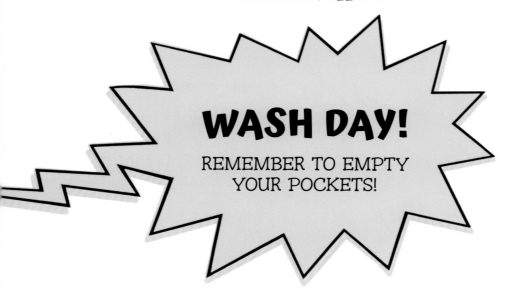

AND LINTY'S LITTLE WORLD TURNED UPSIDE DOWN. LITERALLY.

HERE WE GO!
Look out below!

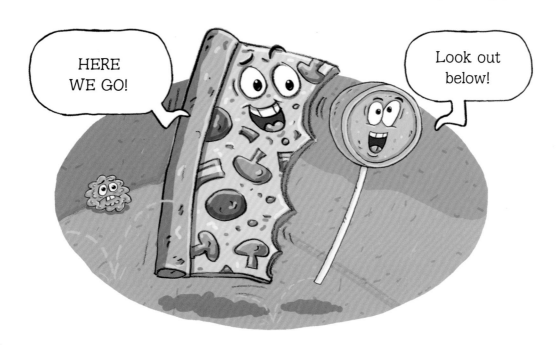

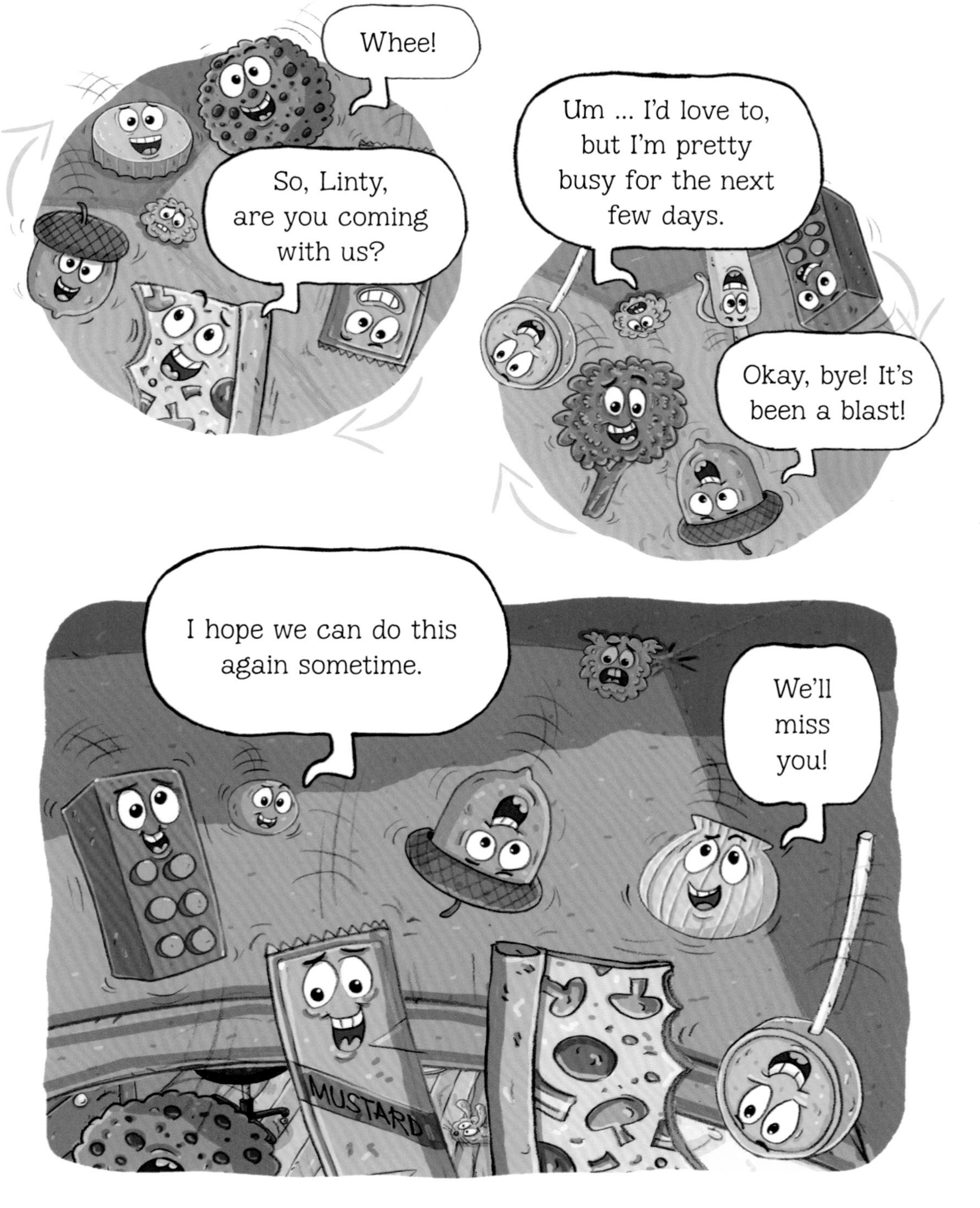
Whee!
So, Linty, are you coming with us?
Um ... I'd love to, but I'm pretty busy for the next few days.
Okay, bye! It's been a blast!
I hope we can do this again sometime.
We'll miss you!
MUSTARD

ALONE AND RIGHT SIDE UP AGAIN, LINTY SETTLED BACK INTO HIS ROUTINE.

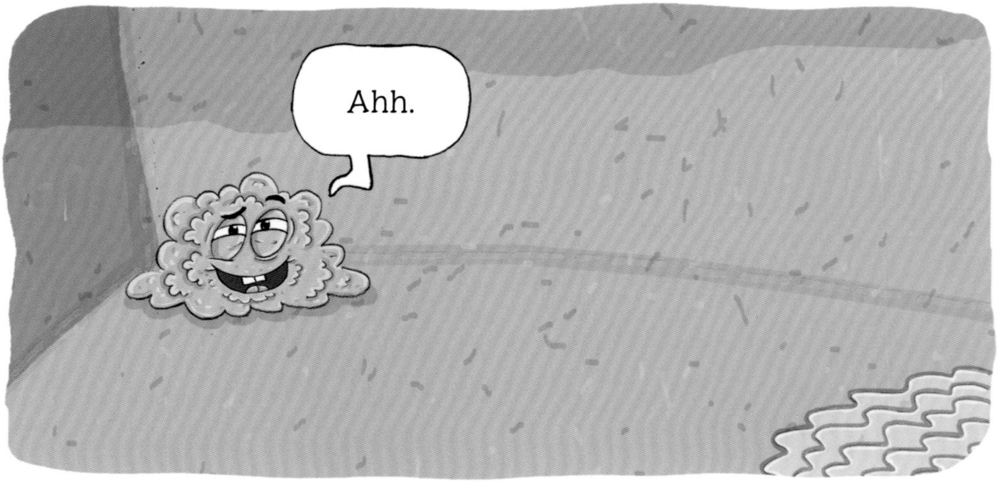
Ahh.

BUT FASTER THAN HE COULD SAY "MARCO POLO," HIS POCKET STARTED FILLING WITH WATER.

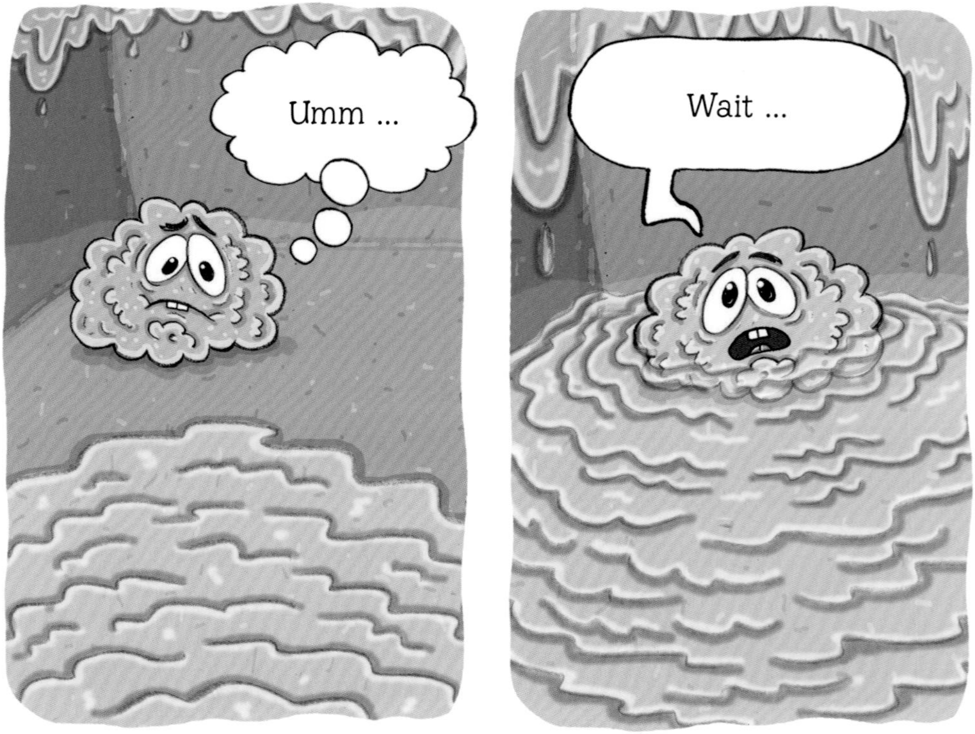
Umm ...
Wait ...

LINTY FLOATED UP, UP, UP ...

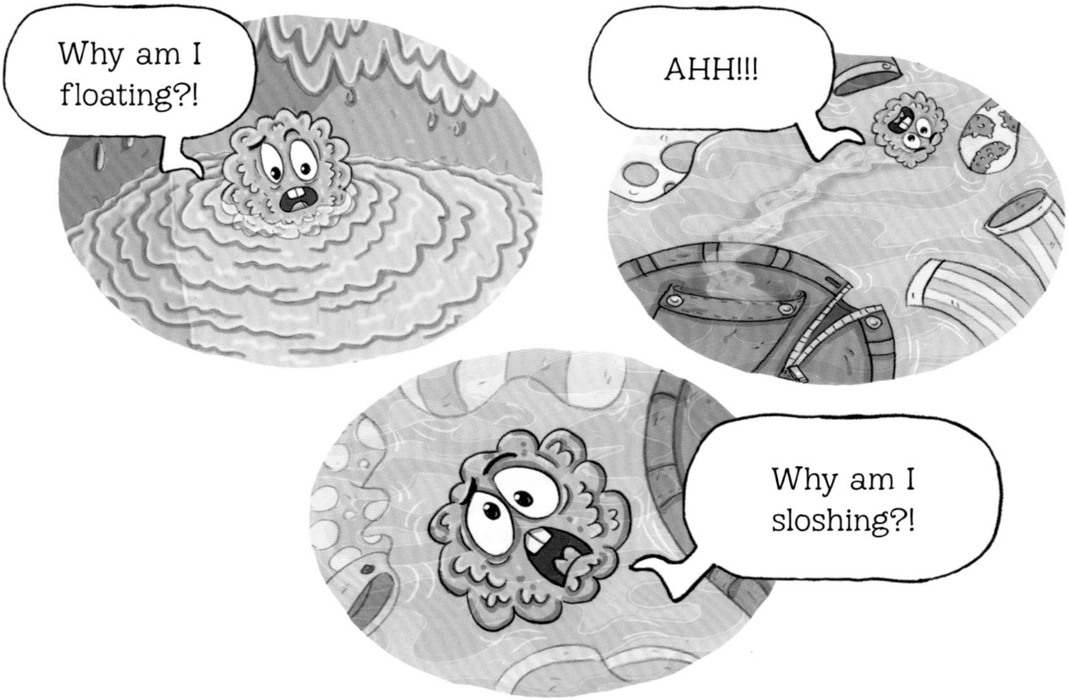
Why am I floating?!
AHH!!!
Why am I sloshing?!

AND OUT OF THE POCKET.

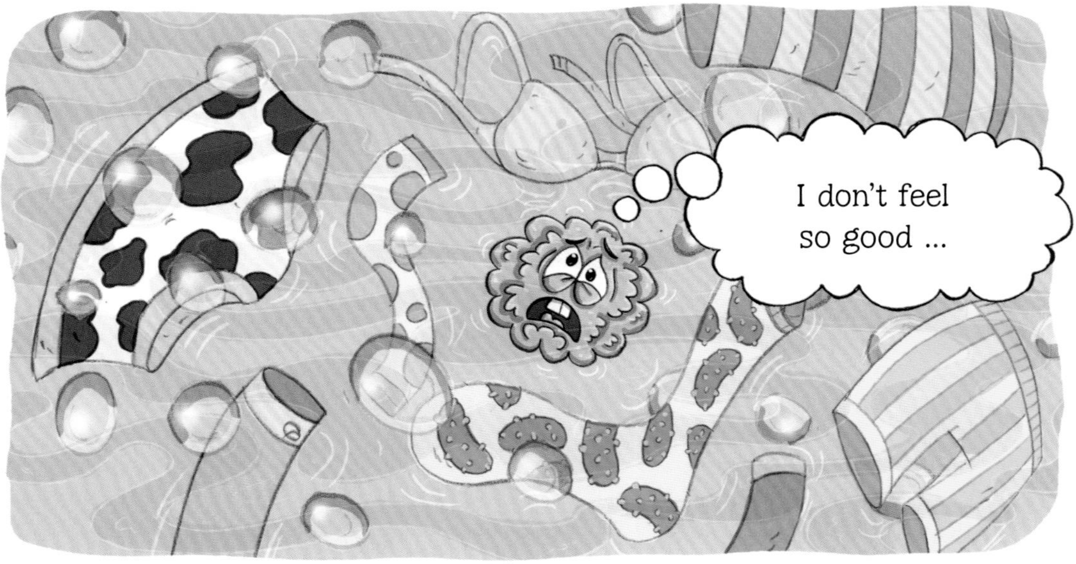
I don't feel so good ...

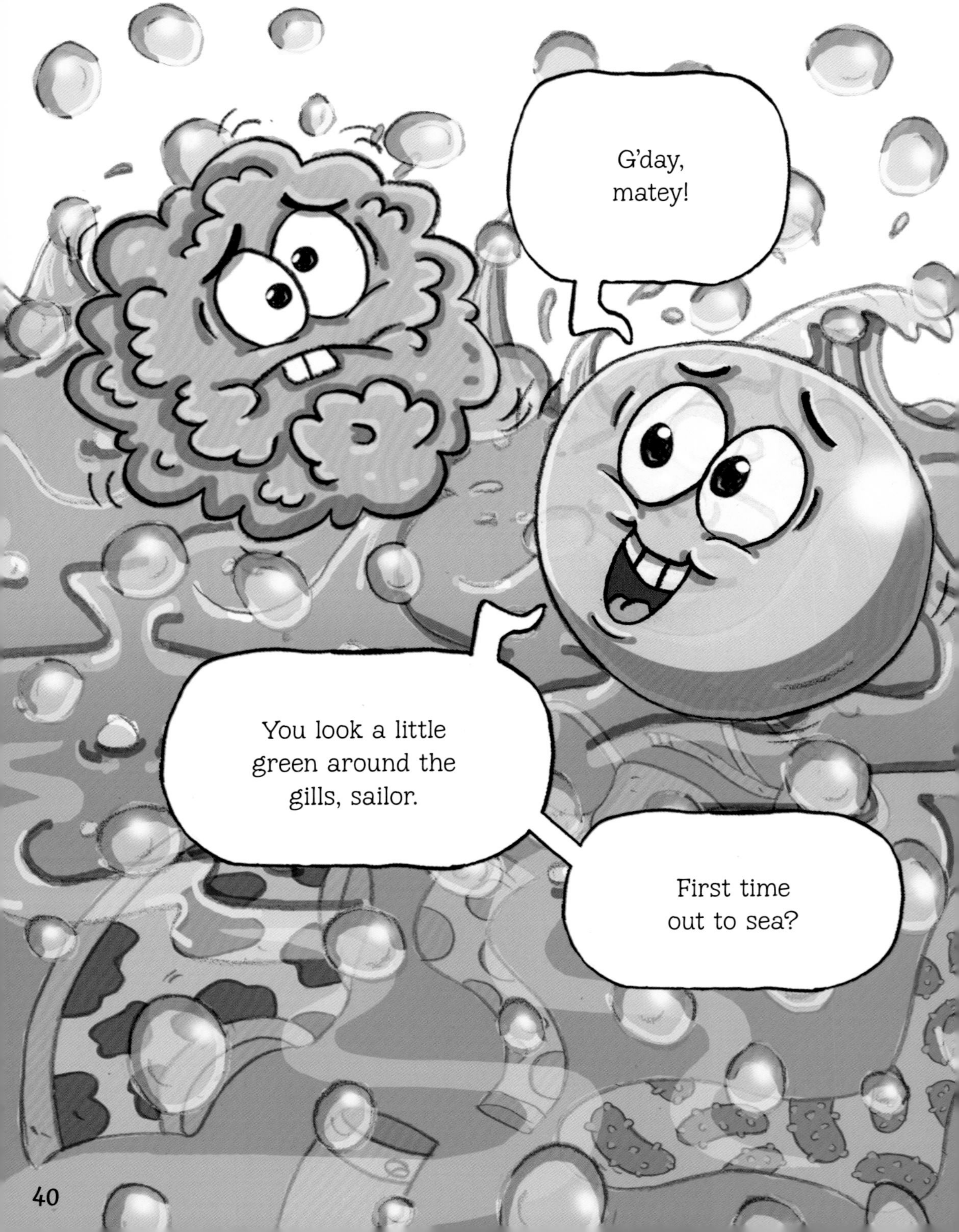
G'day, matey!
You look a little green around the gills, sailor.
First time out to sea?

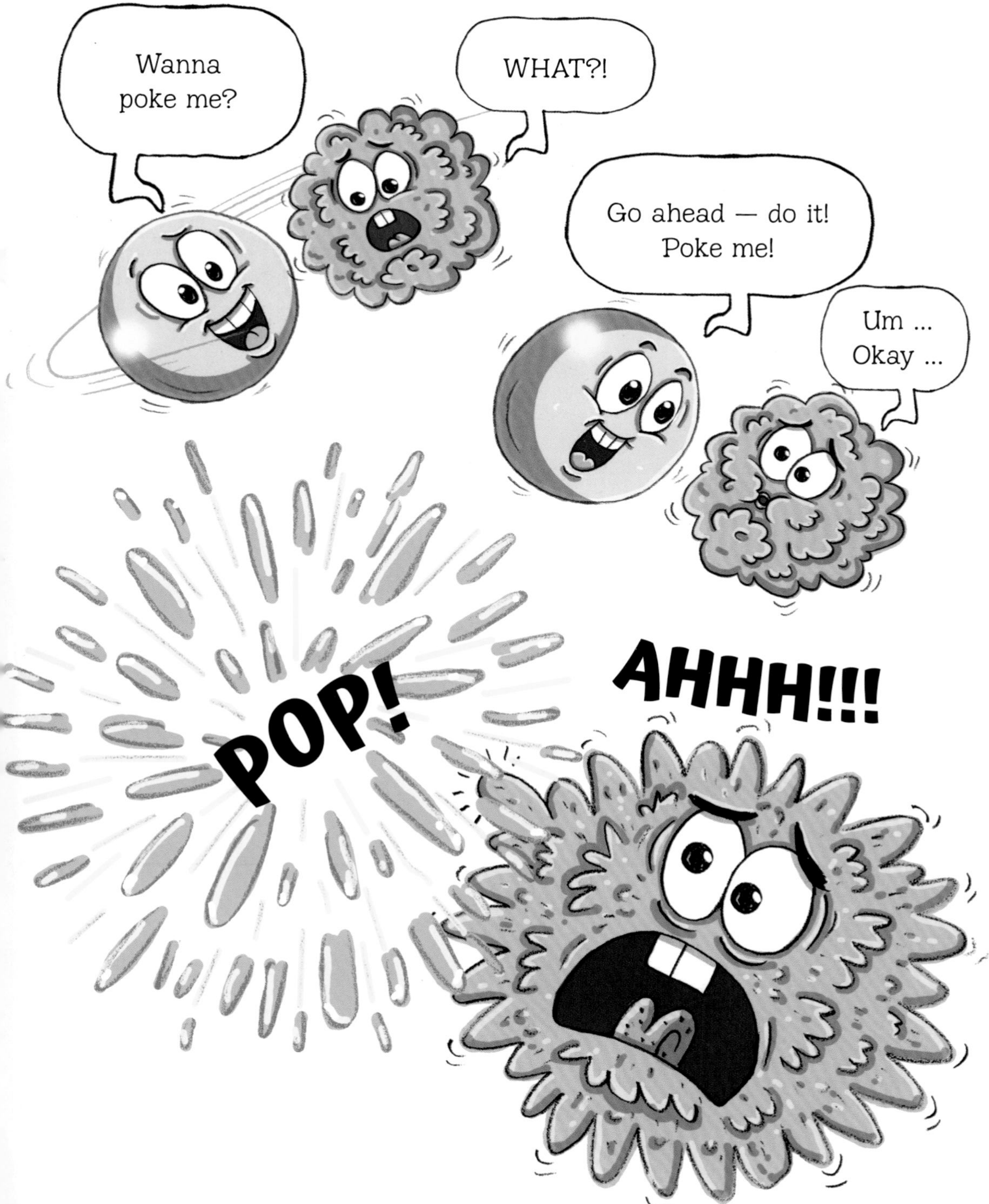
Wanna poke me?
WHAT?!
Go ahead — do it! Poke me!
Um ... Okay ...
POP!
AHHH!!!

AFTER A STOMACH-LURCHING SPIN ...

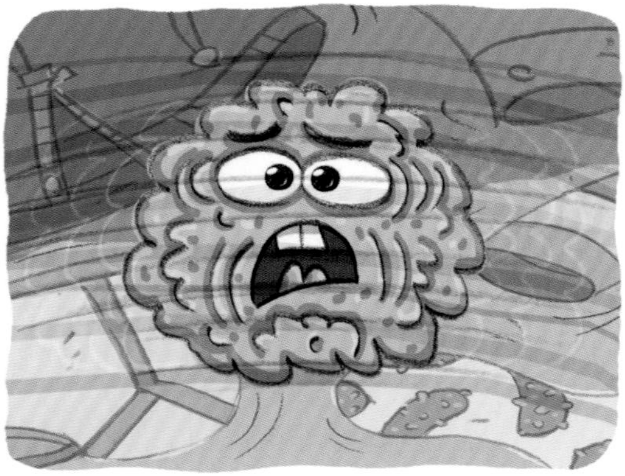

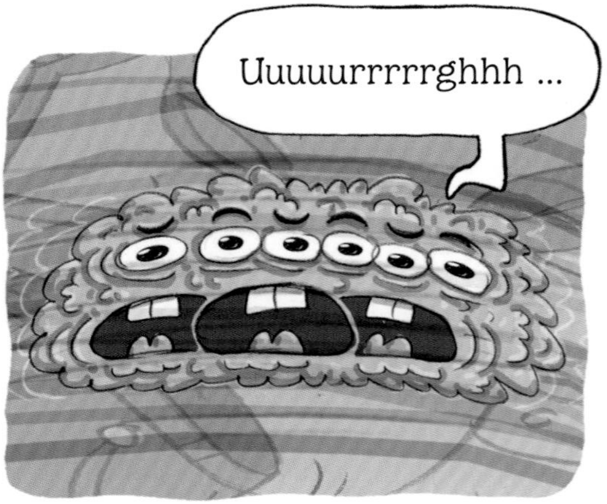
Uuuuurrrrrghhh ...

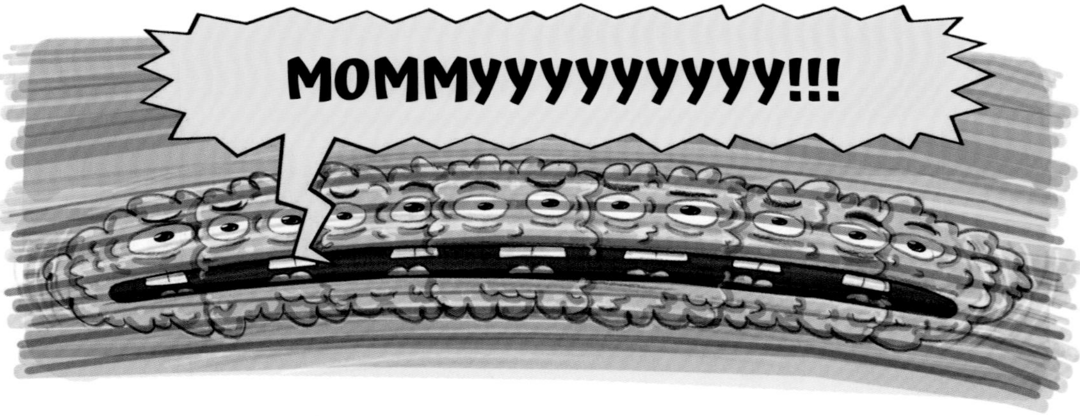
MOMMYYYYYYYYYY!!!

LINTY WAS TOSSED INTO THE DRYER.

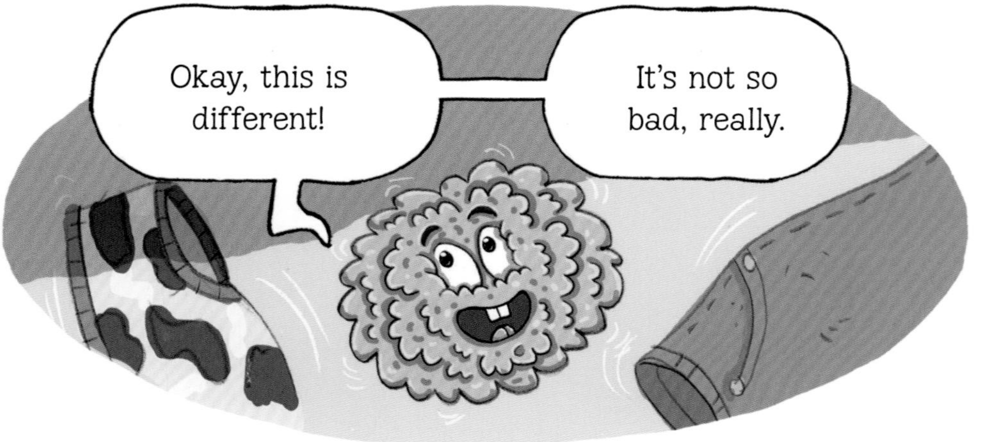
Okay, this is different!
It's not so bad, really.

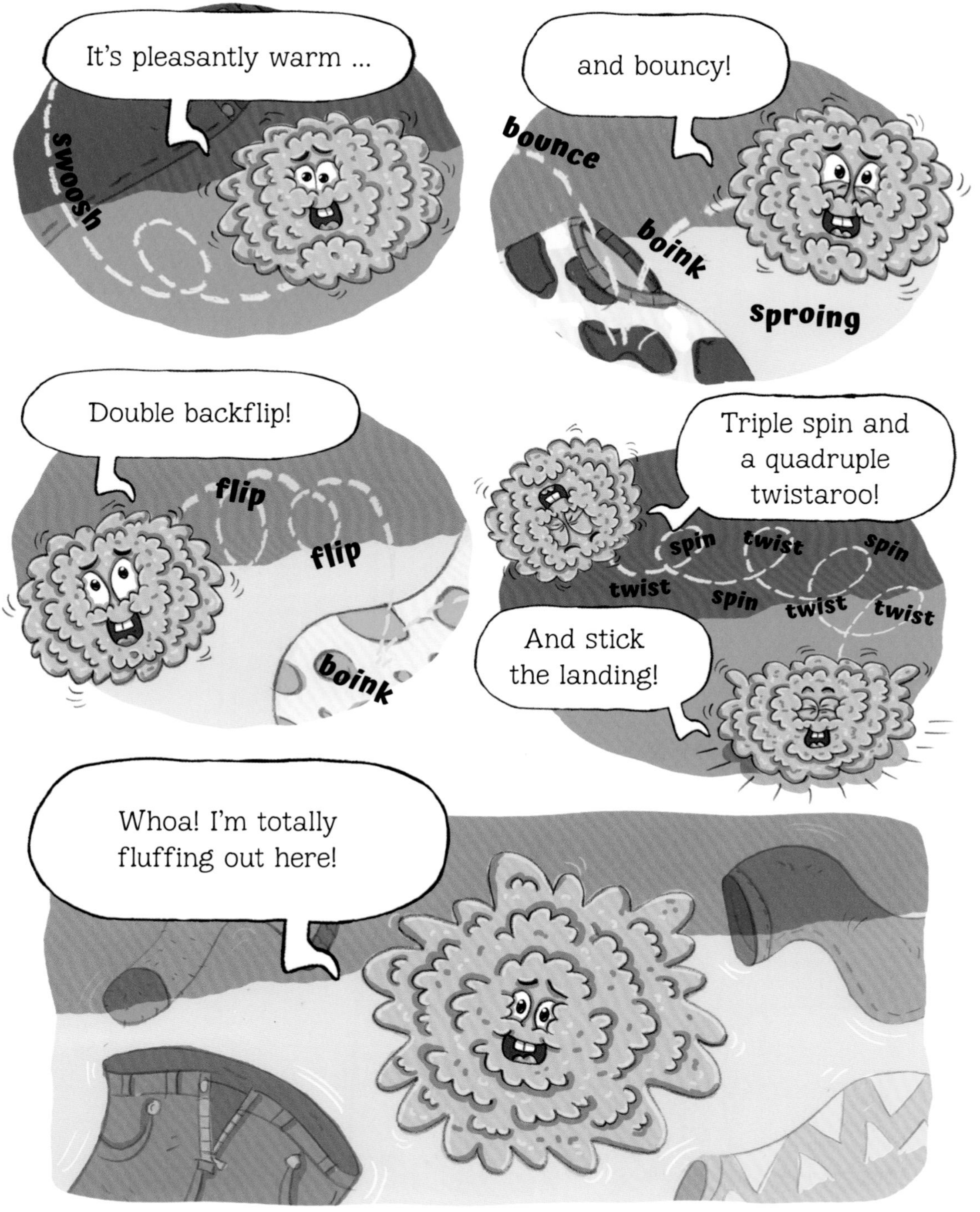
It's pleasantly warm ...
swoosh
and bouncy!
bounce
boink
sproing
Double backflip!
flip
flip
boink
Triple spin and a quadruple twistaroo!
spin
twist
spin
twist
spin
twist
twist
And stick the landing!
Whoa! I'm totally fluffing out here!

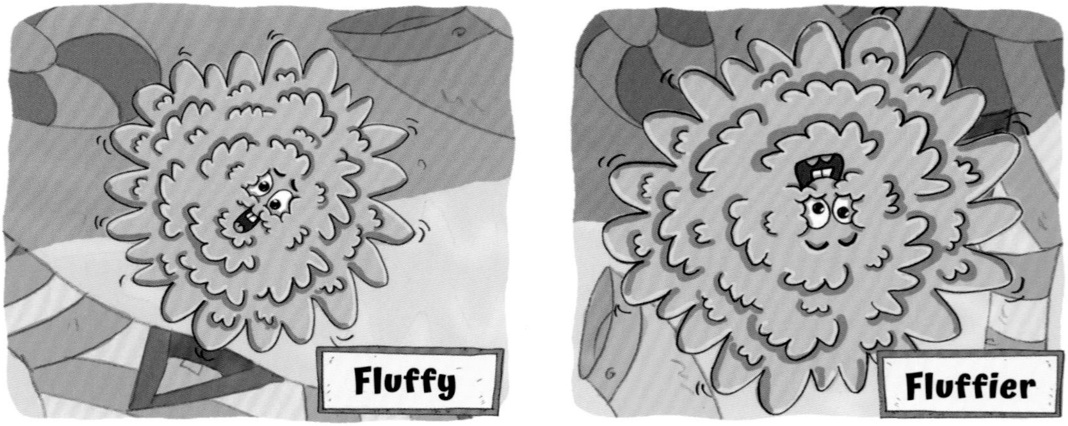
Fluffy
Fluffier

THEN SOMETHING CAUGHT LINTY'S EYE ...

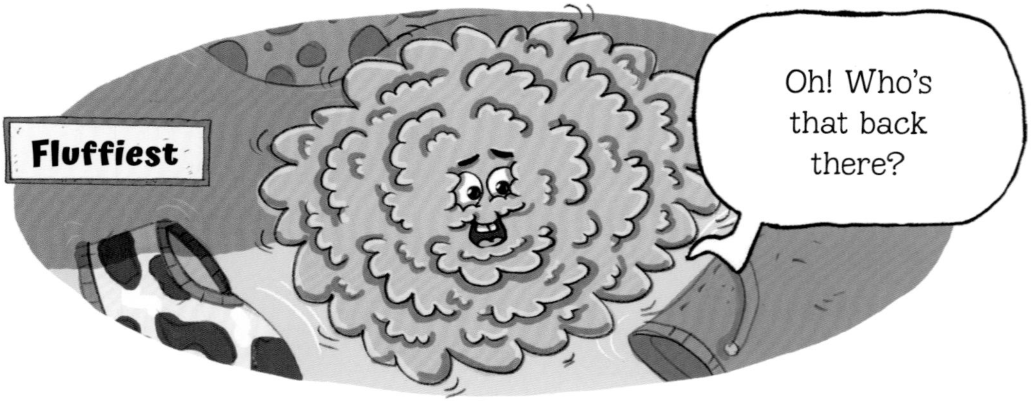
Fluffiest
Oh! Who's that back there?

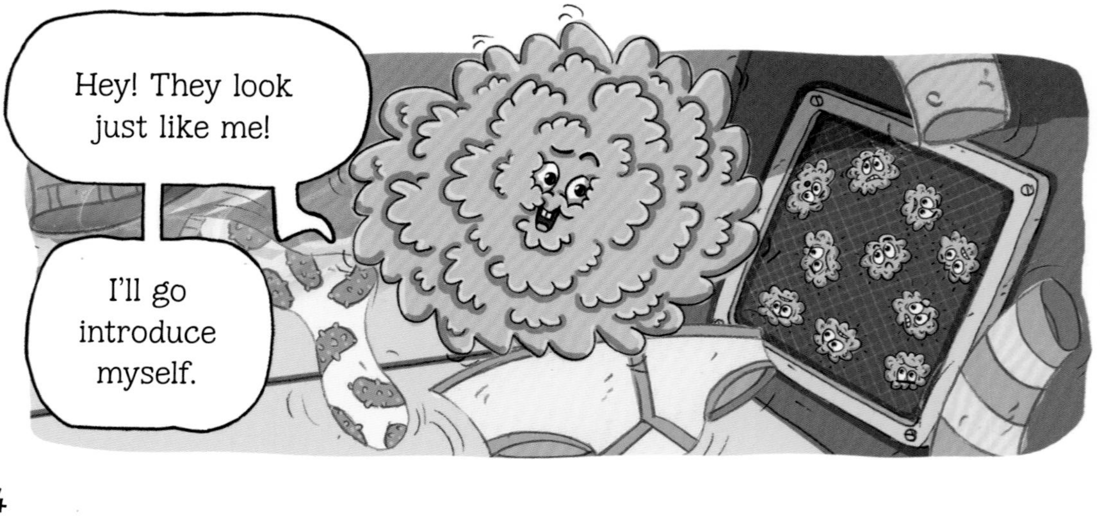
Hey! They look just like me!
I'll go introduce myself.

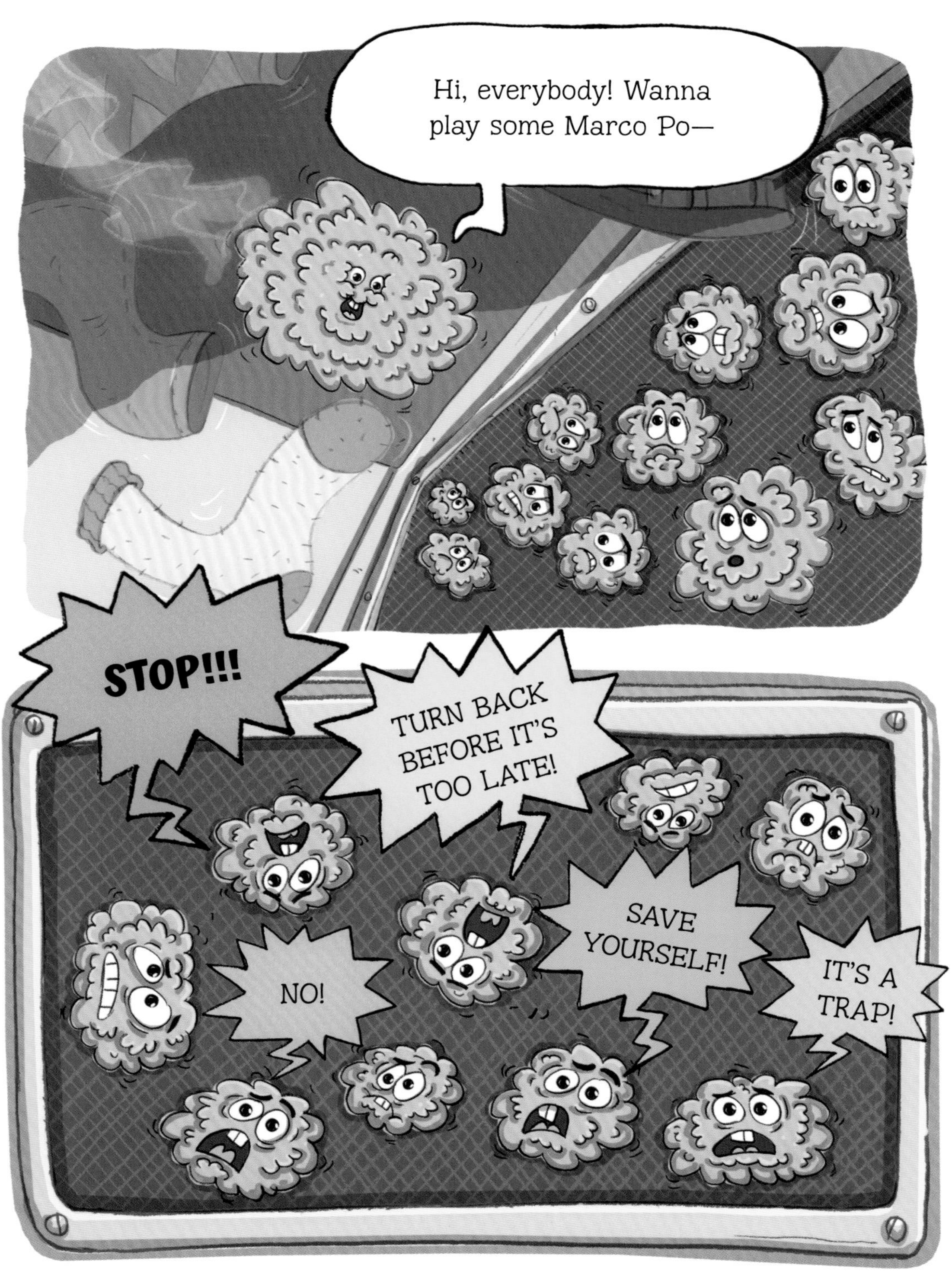
Hi, everybody! Wanna play some Marco Po—
STOP!!!
TURN BACK BEFORE IT'S TOO LATE!
NO!
SAVE YOURSELF!
IT'S A TRAP!

JUST AS LINTY WAS ABOUT TO GET SUCKED INTO THE LINT TRAP ...

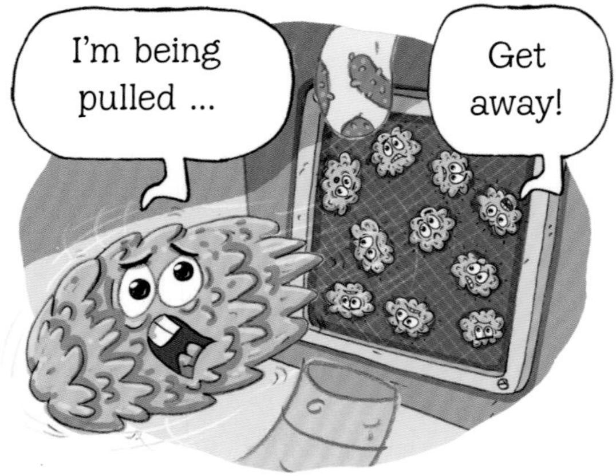
I'm being pulled ...
Get away!

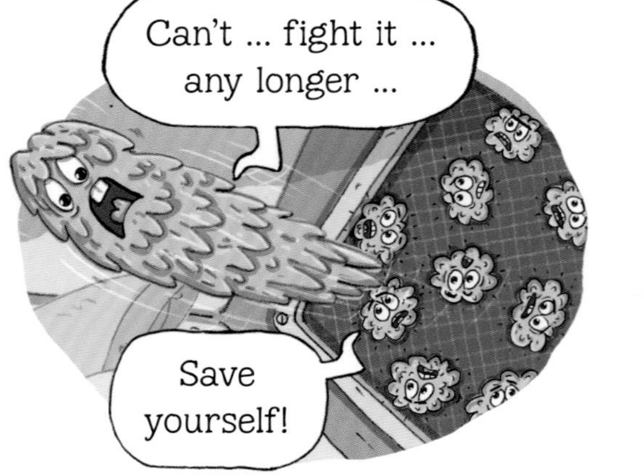
Can't ... fight it ... any longer ...
Save yourself!

THE JEANS FLEW PAST AND HE GRABBED ON.

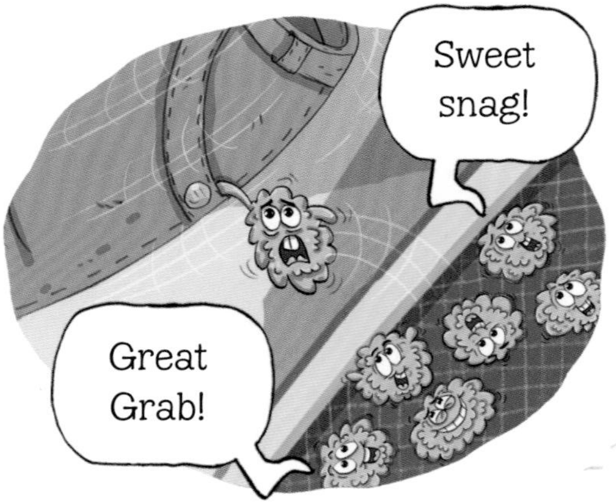
Sweet snag!
Great Grab!

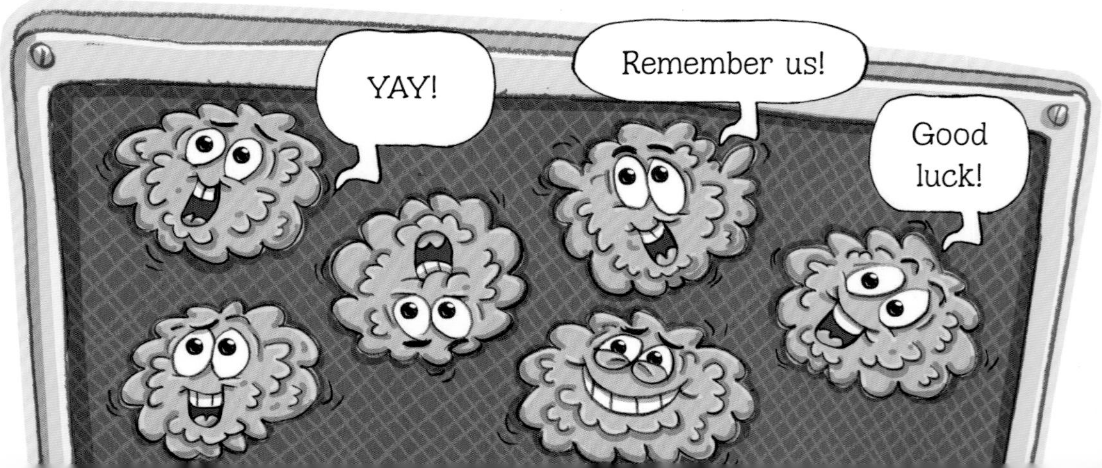
YAY!
Remember us!
Good luck!

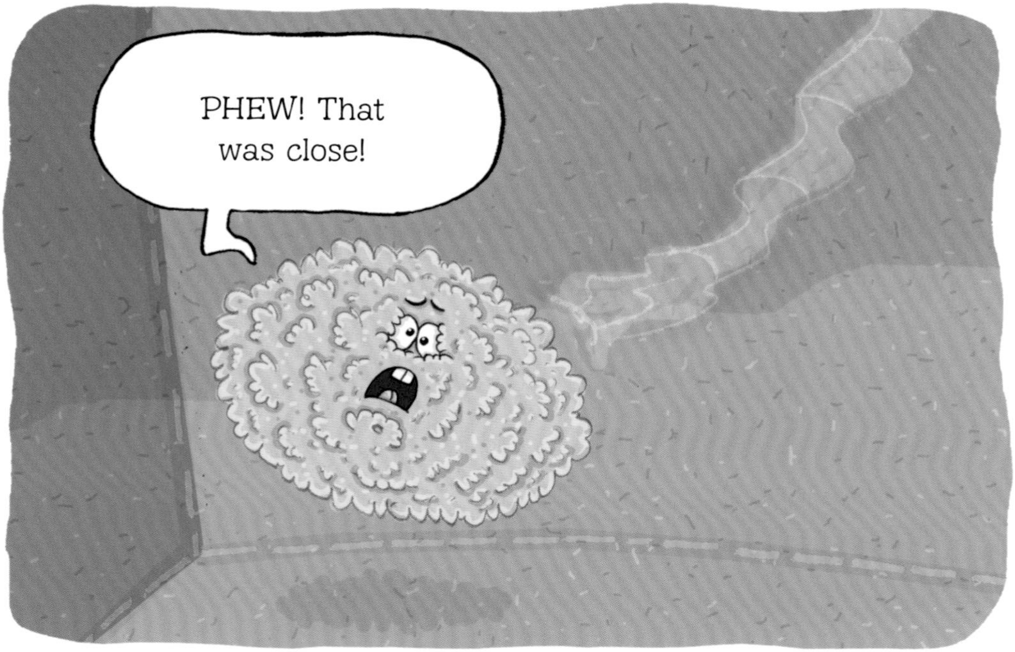
PHEW! That was close!

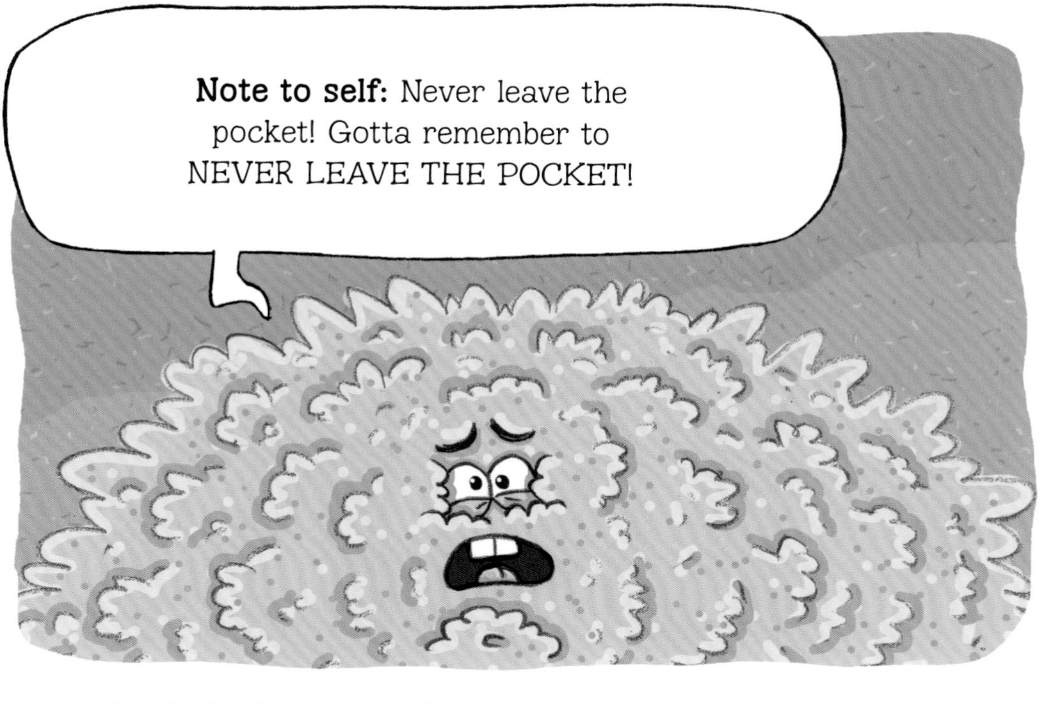
Note to self: Never leave the pocket! Gotta remember to NEVER LEAVE THE POCKET!

AND SO, EVERYTHING WENT BACK TO THE WAY IT WAS BEFORE.

(ALMOST.)

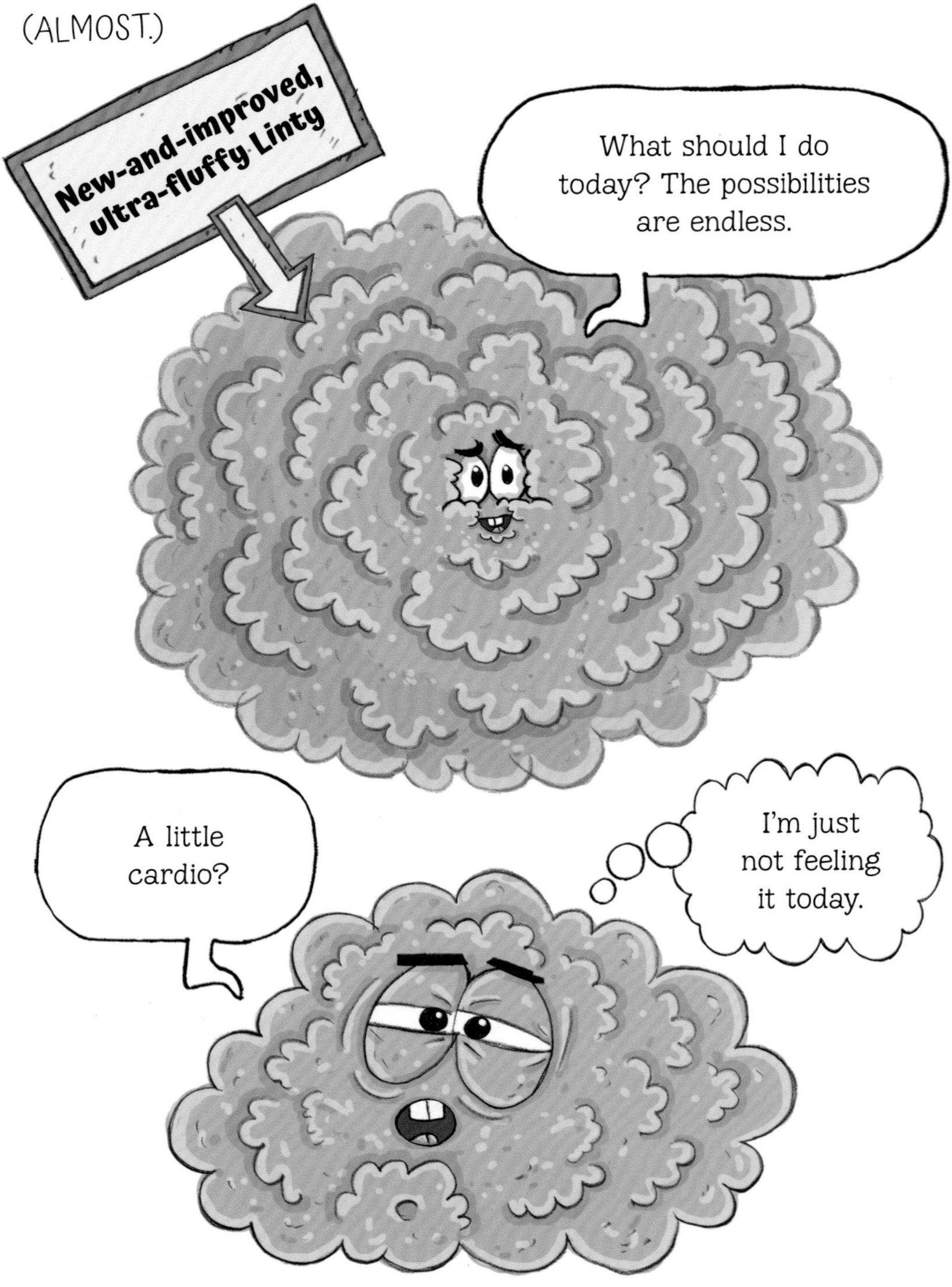
New-and-improved, ultra-fluffy Linty
What should I do today? The possibilities are endless.
A little cardio?
I'm just not feeling it today.

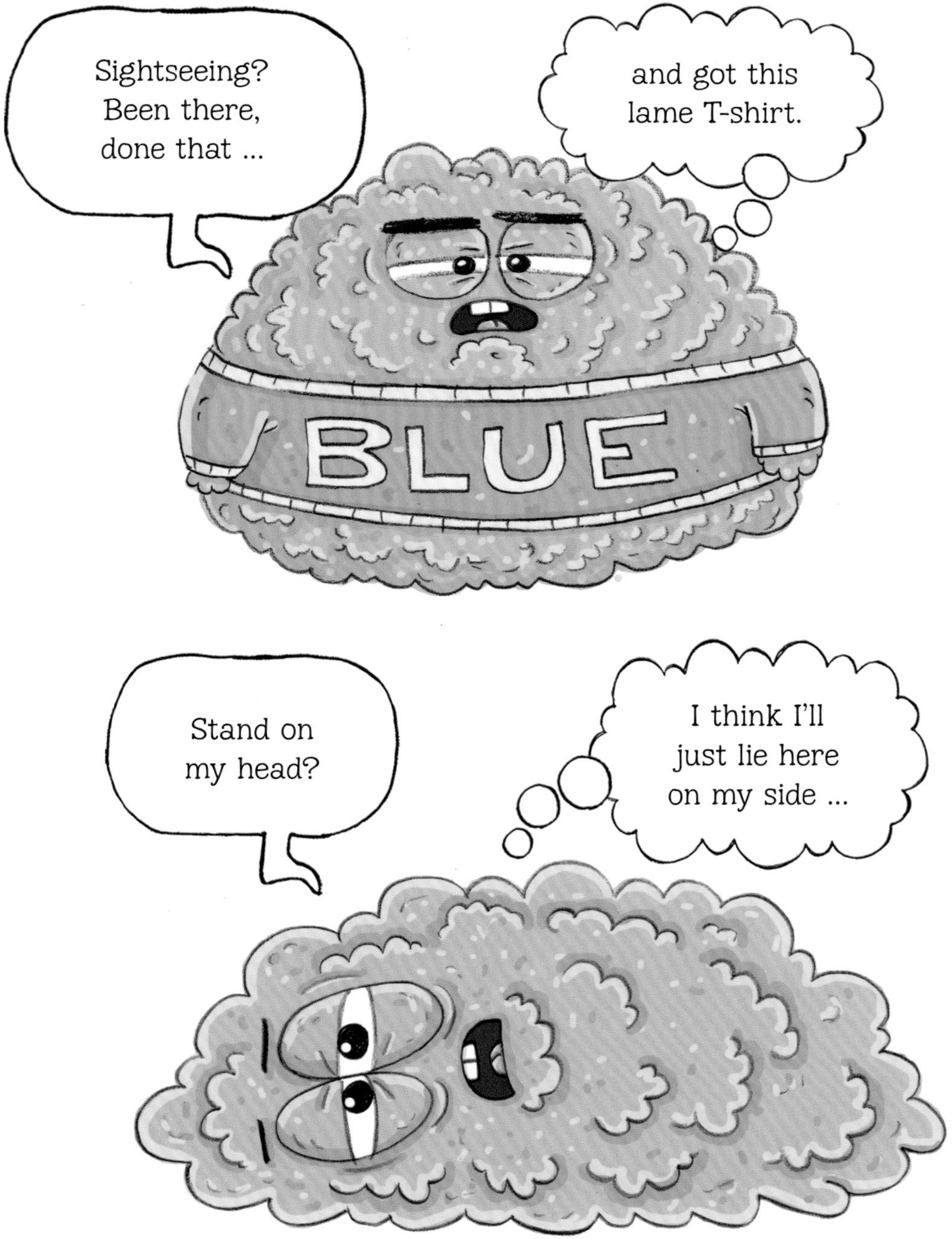
Sightseeing? Been there, done that ...
and got this lame T-shirt.
BLUE
Stand on my head?
I think I'll just lie here on my side ...

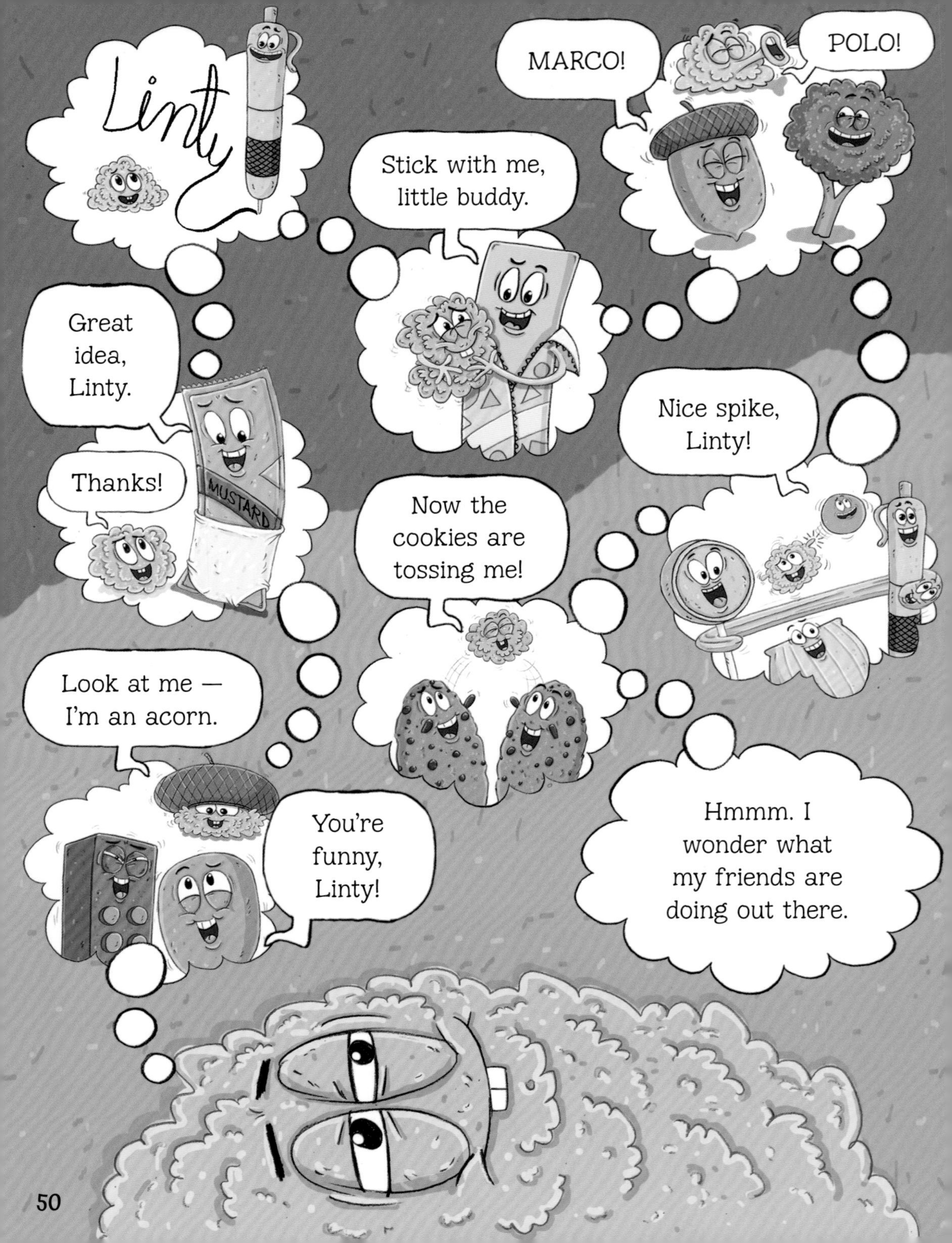
Linty
MARCO!
POLO!
Stick with me, little buddy.
Great idea, Linty.
Thanks!
MUSTARD
Nice spike, Linty!
Now the cookies are tossing me!
Look at me — I'm an acorn.
You're funny, Linty!
Hmmm. I wonder what my friends are doing out there.

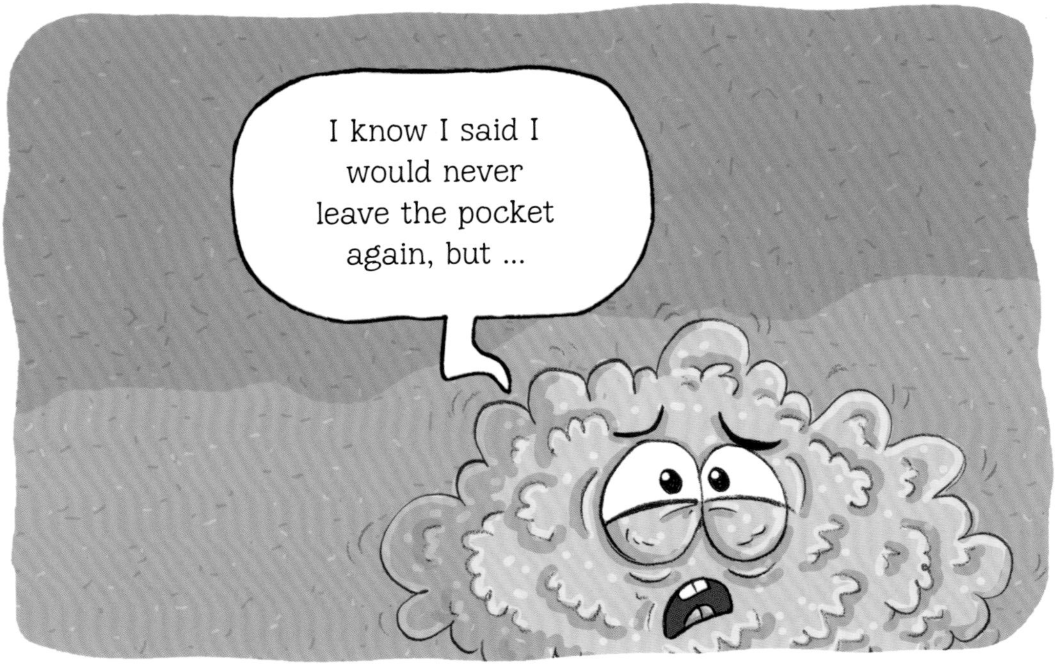
I know I said I would never leave the pocket again, but ...

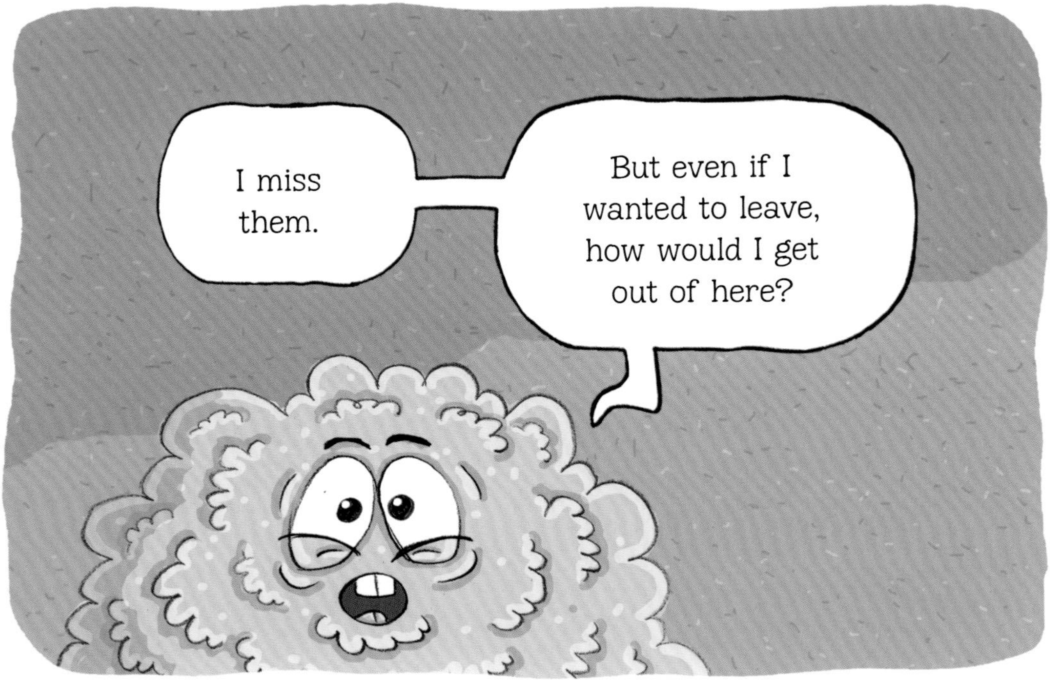
I miss them.
But even if I wanted to leave, how would I get out of here?

LINTY HEMMED AND HAWED AND HAWED AND HEMMED.

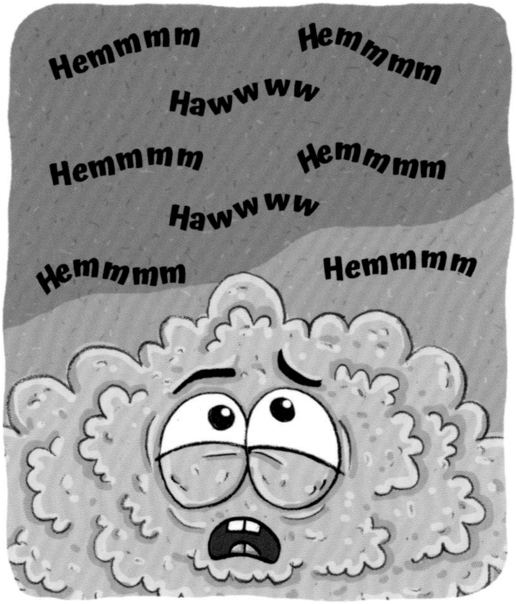
Hemmmm
Hemmmm
Hawwww
Hemmmm
Hemmmm
Hawwww
Hemmmm
Hemmmm

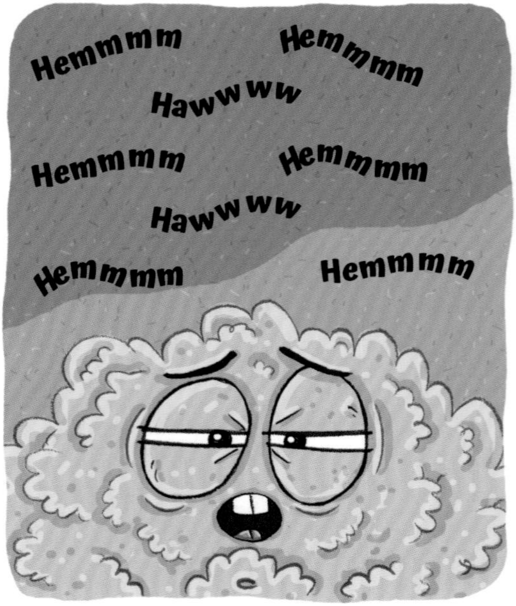
Hemmmm
Hemmmm
Hawwww
Hemmmm
Hemmmm
Hawwww
Hemmmm
Hemmmm

AND THEN!

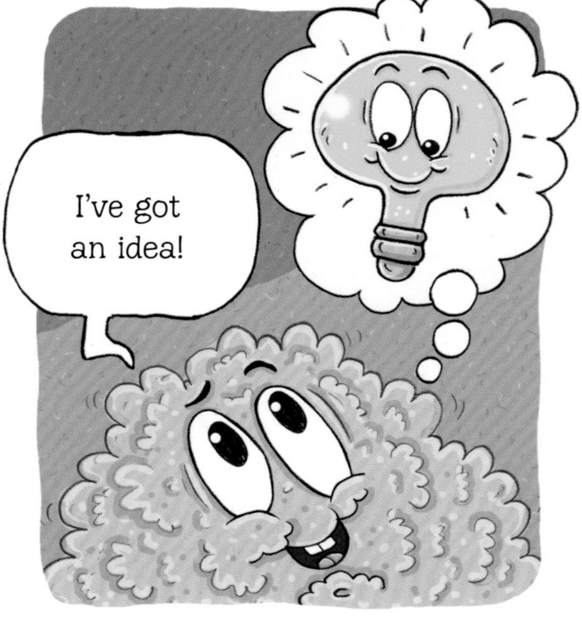
I've got an idea!

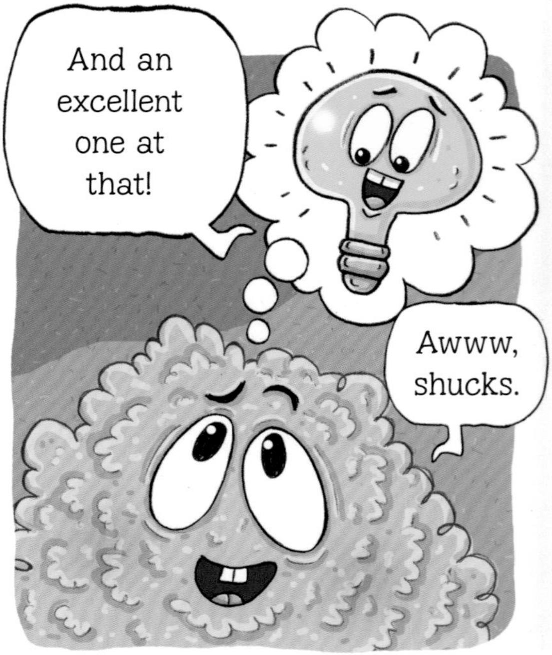
And an excellent one at that!
Awww, shucks.

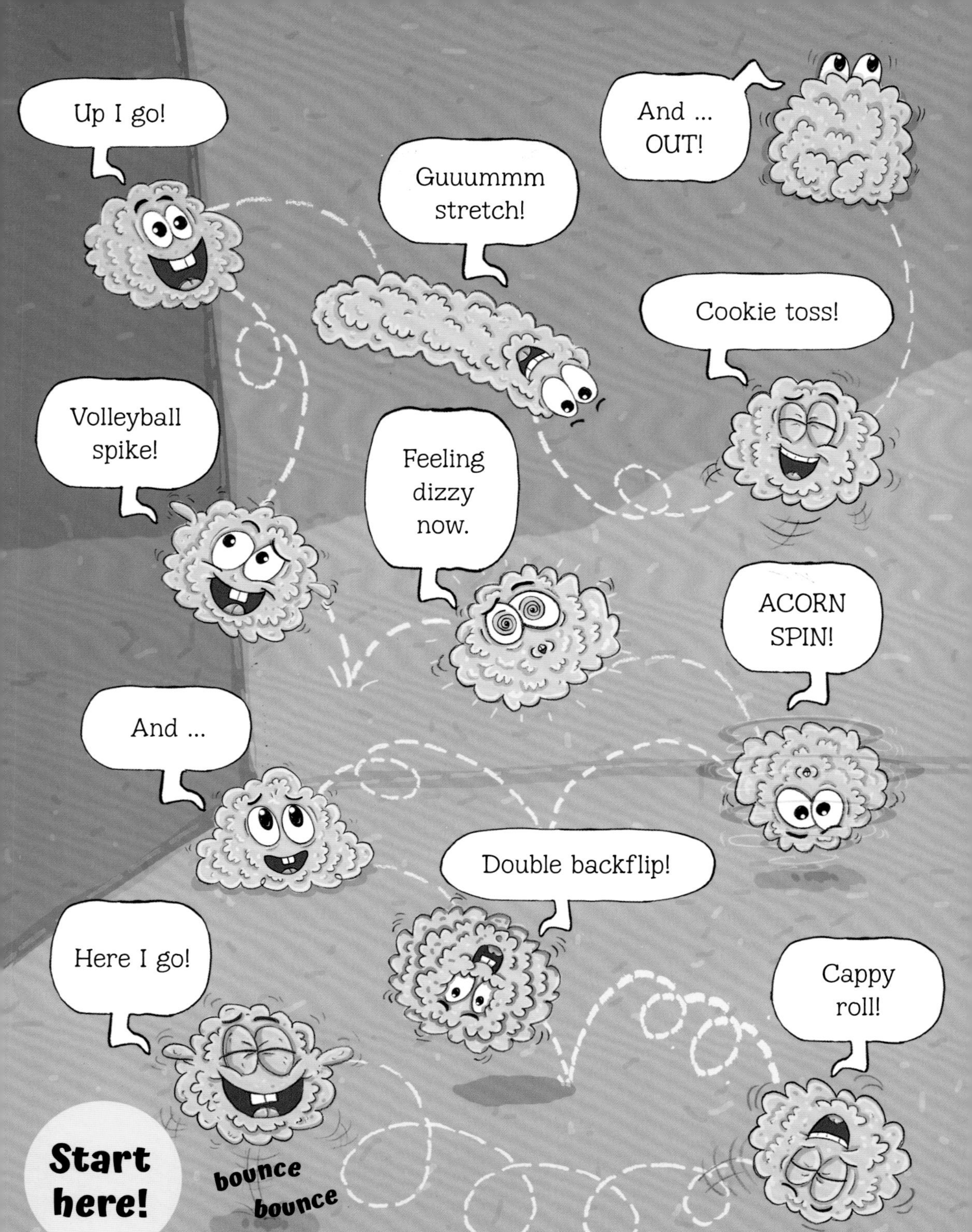
Start here!
bounce
bounce
Here I go!
And ...
Volleyball spike!
Up I go!
Guuummm stretch!
Feeling dizzy now.
Double backflip!
Cappy roll!
ACORN SPIN!
Cookie toss!
And ... OUT!

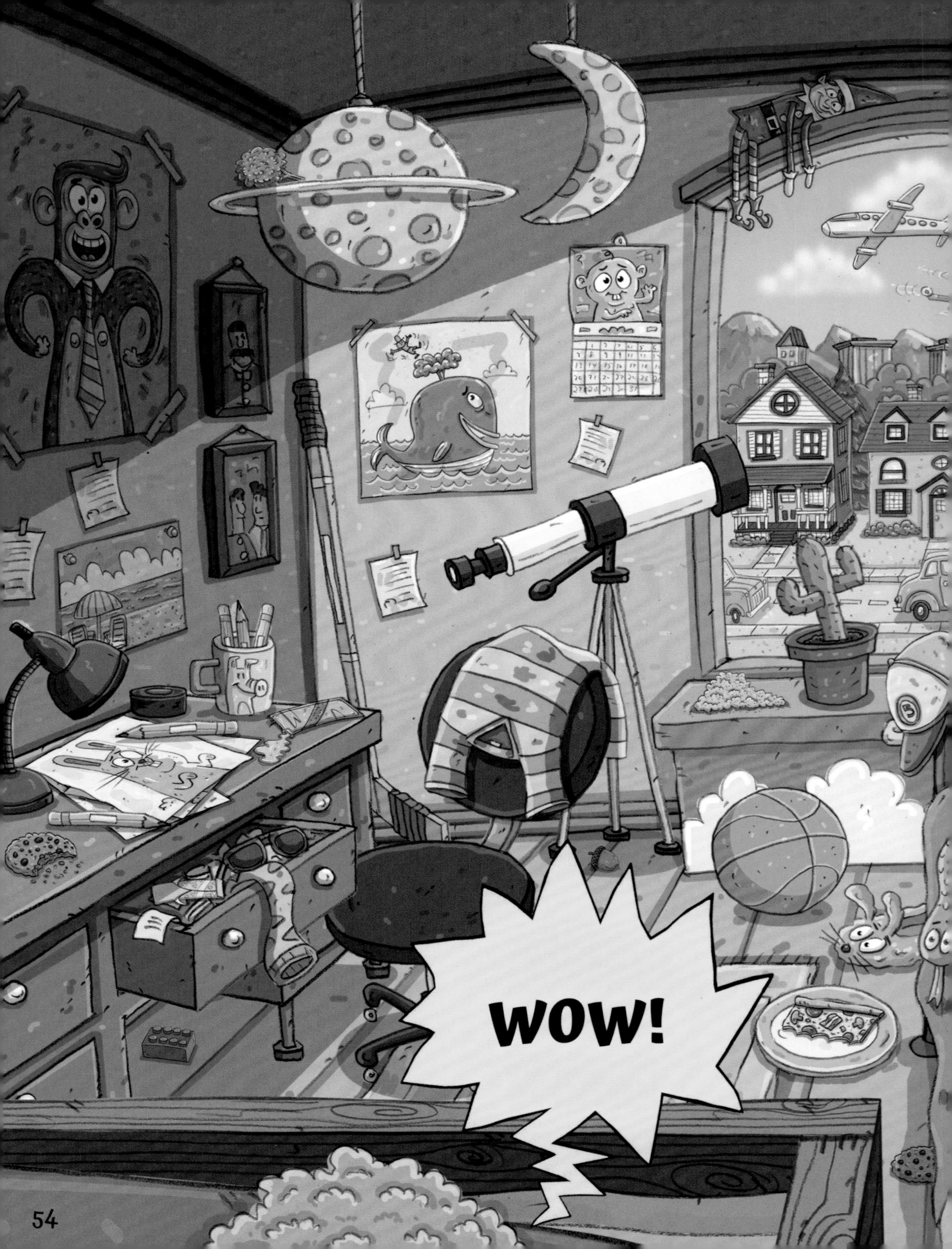
WOW!

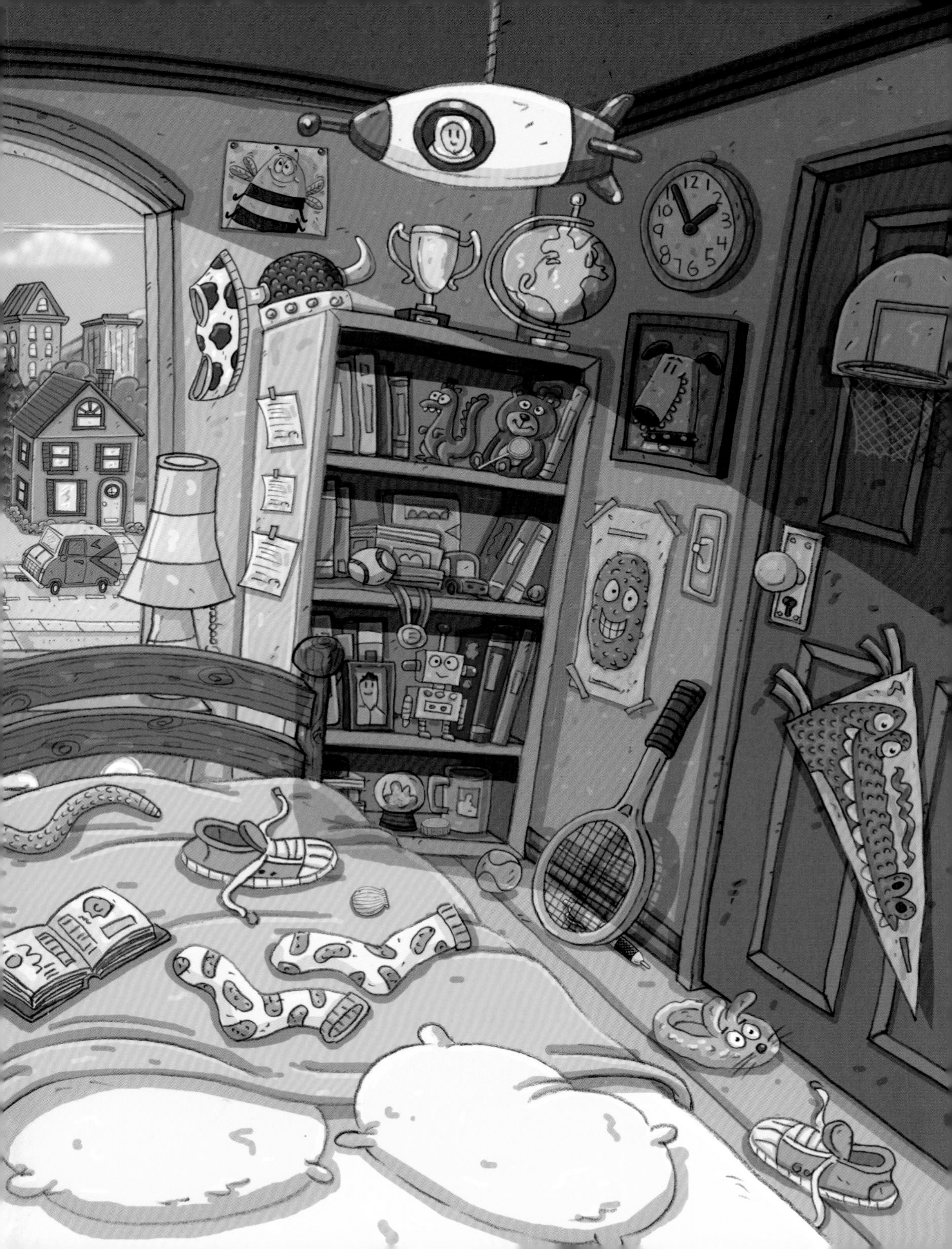

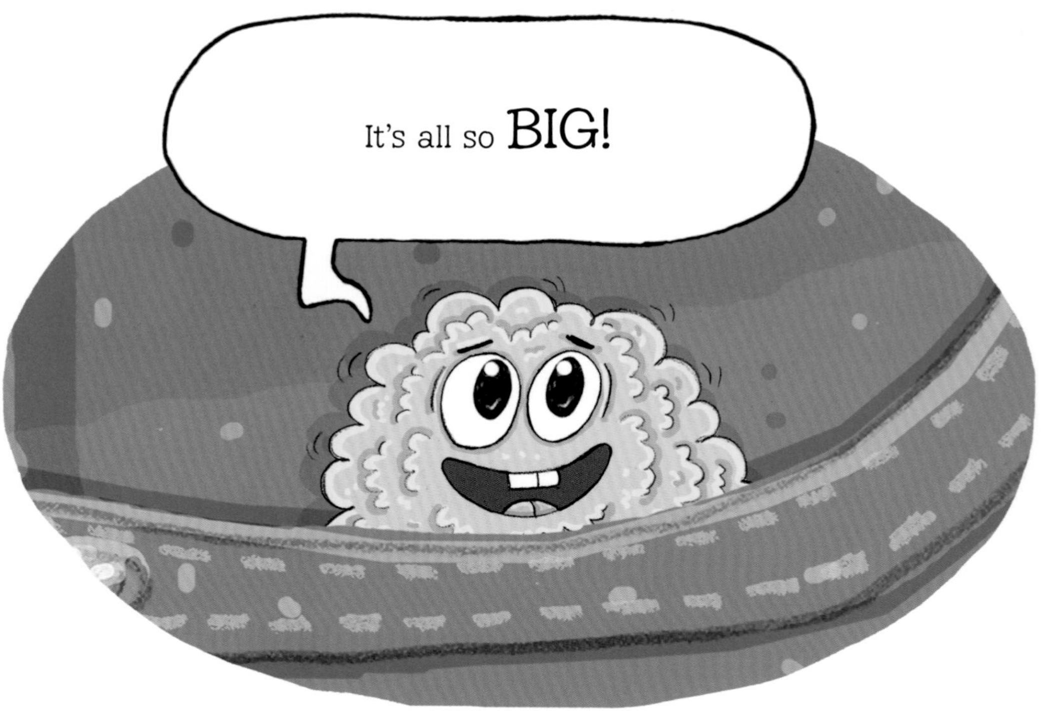
It's all so BIG!

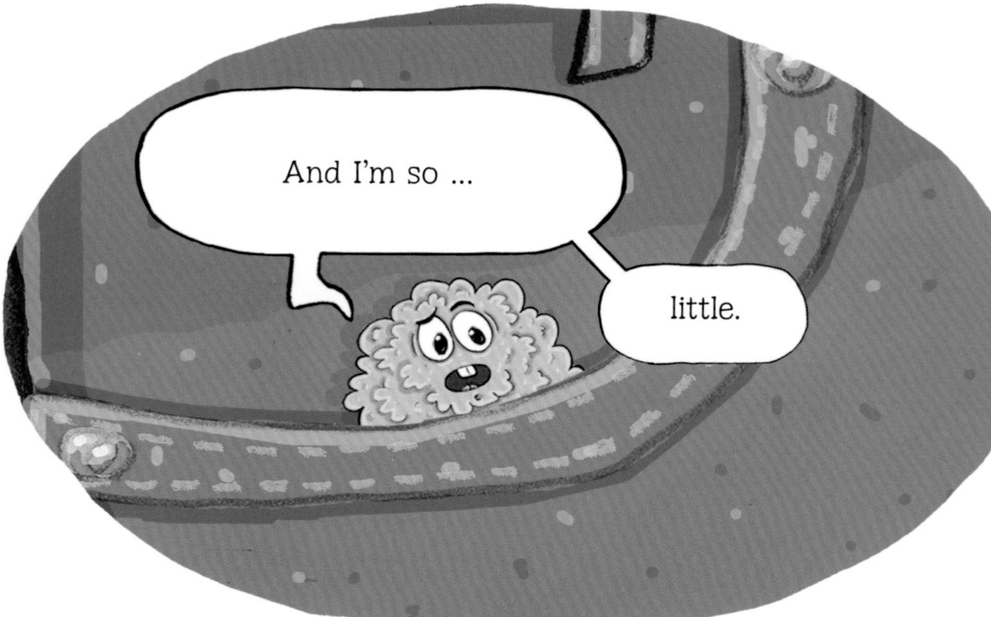
And I'm so ...
little.

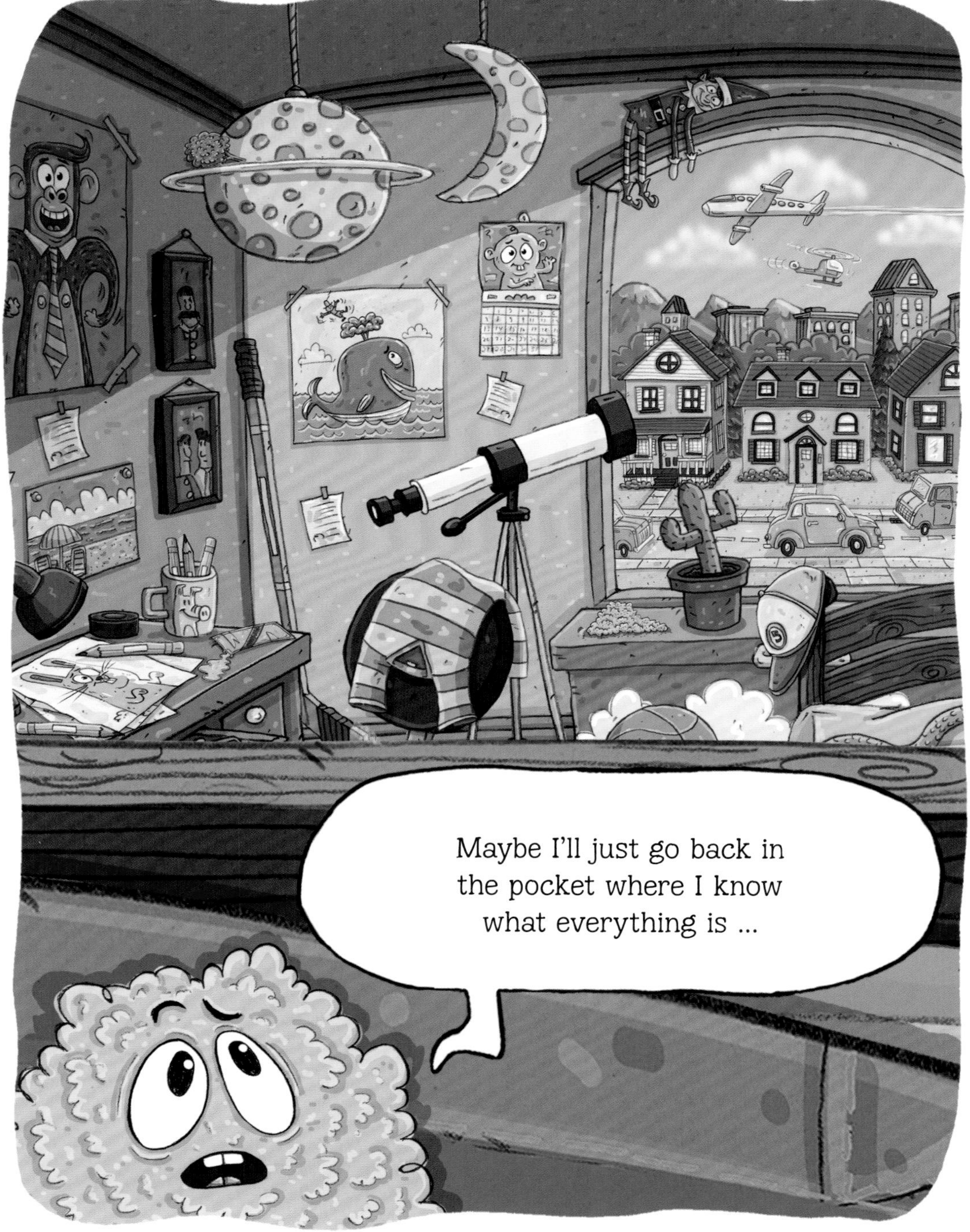
Maybe I'll just go back in the pocket where I know what everything is ...

LINTY SLID BACK DOWN INTO THE POCKET WHERE IT WAS SAFE.

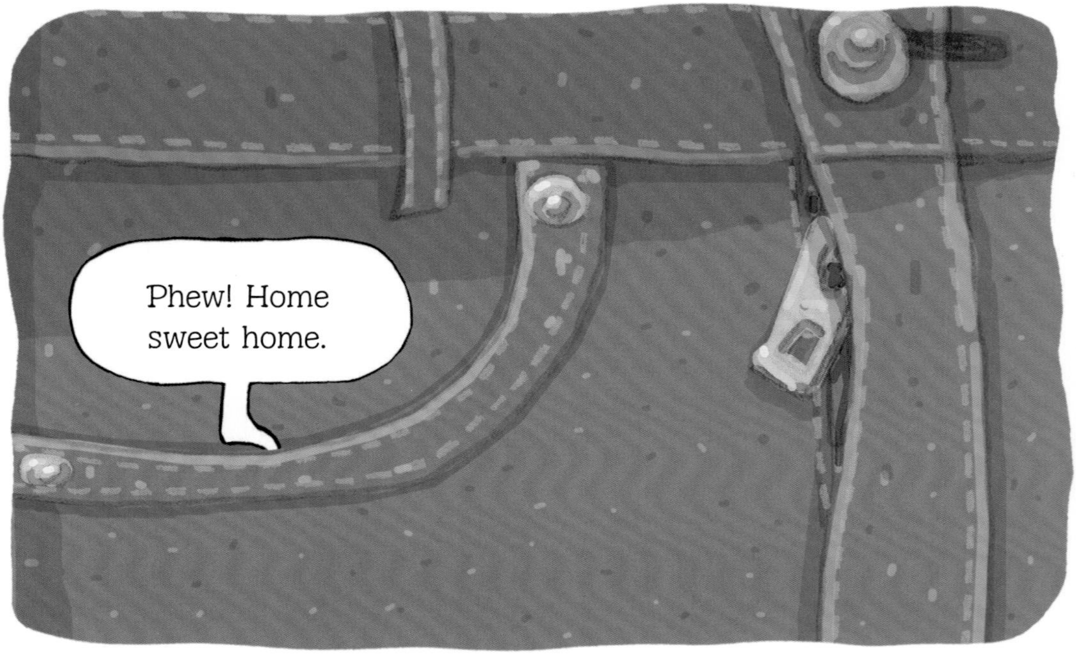
Phew! Home sweet home.

BUT THEN HE HAD A THOUGHT ...

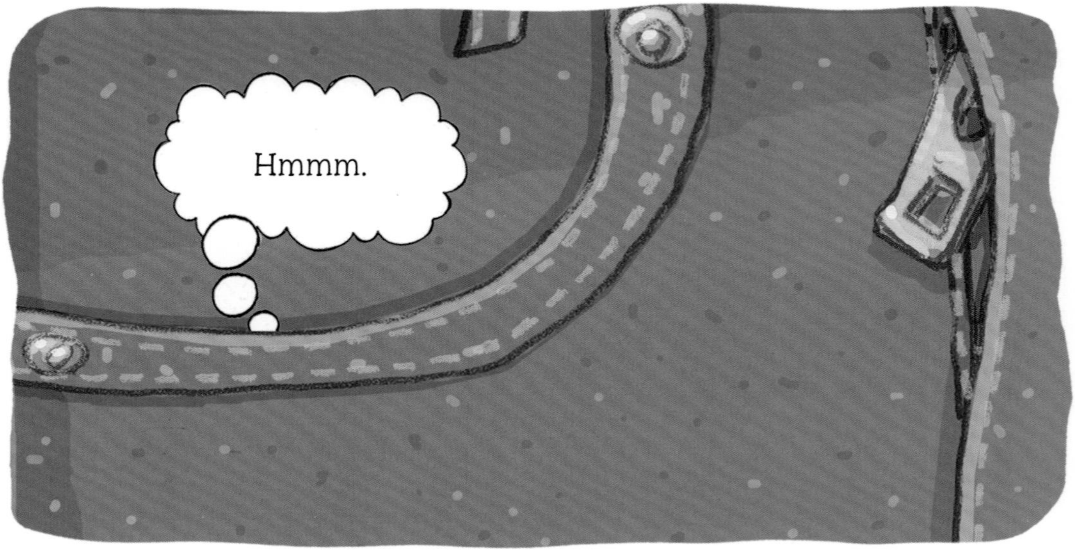
Hmmm.

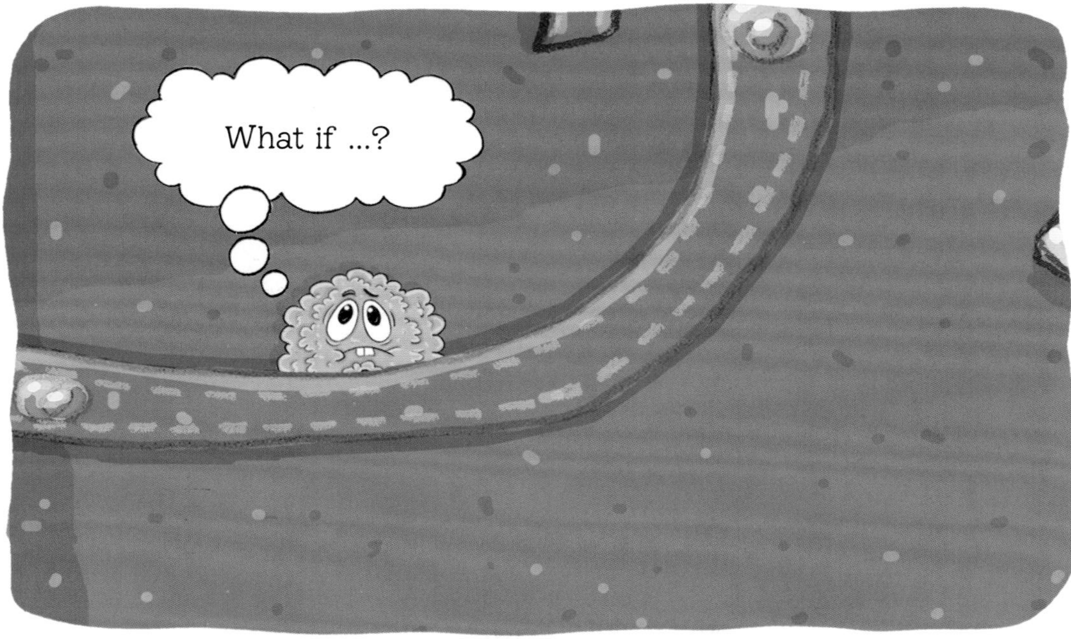
What if ...?

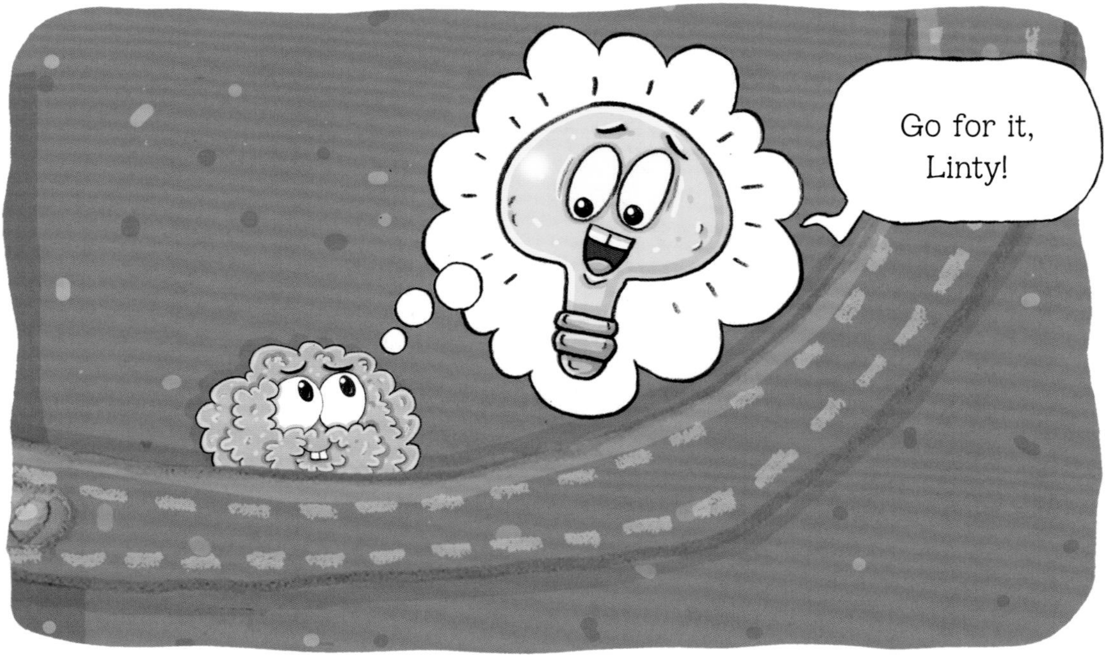
Go for it, Linty!

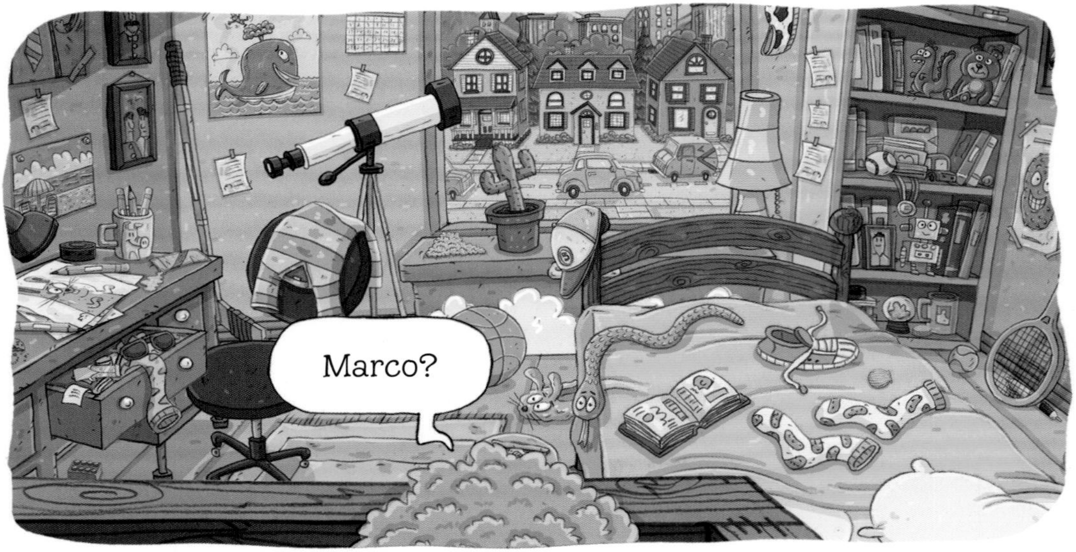
Marco?

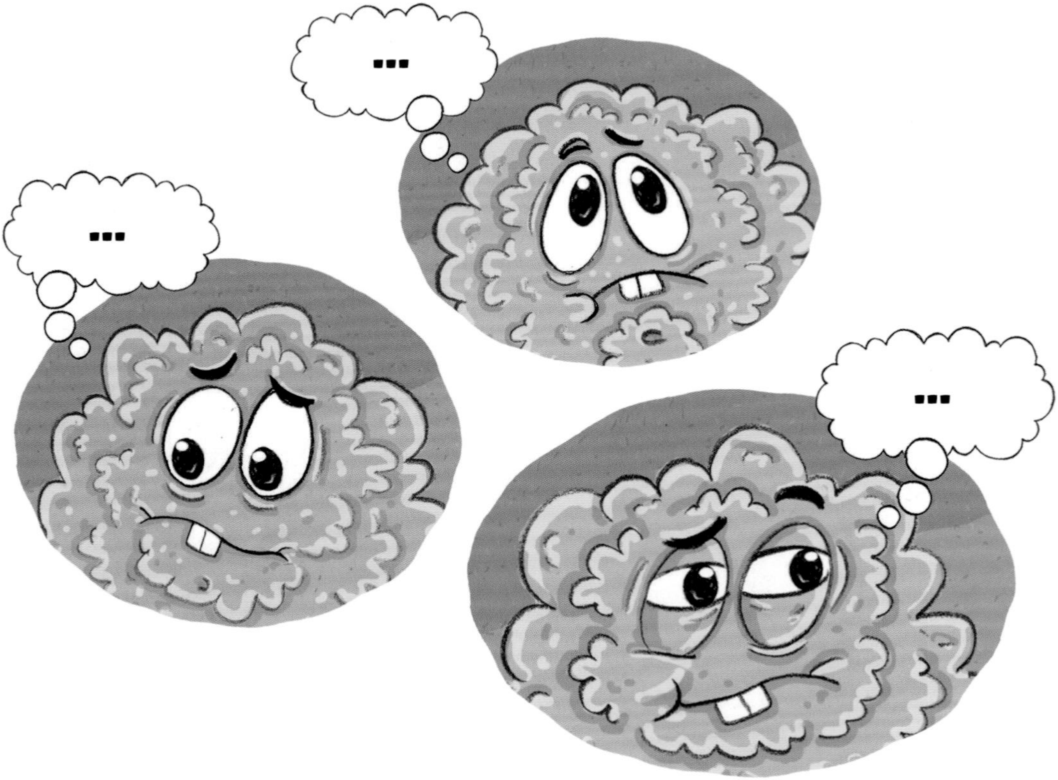
...
...
...

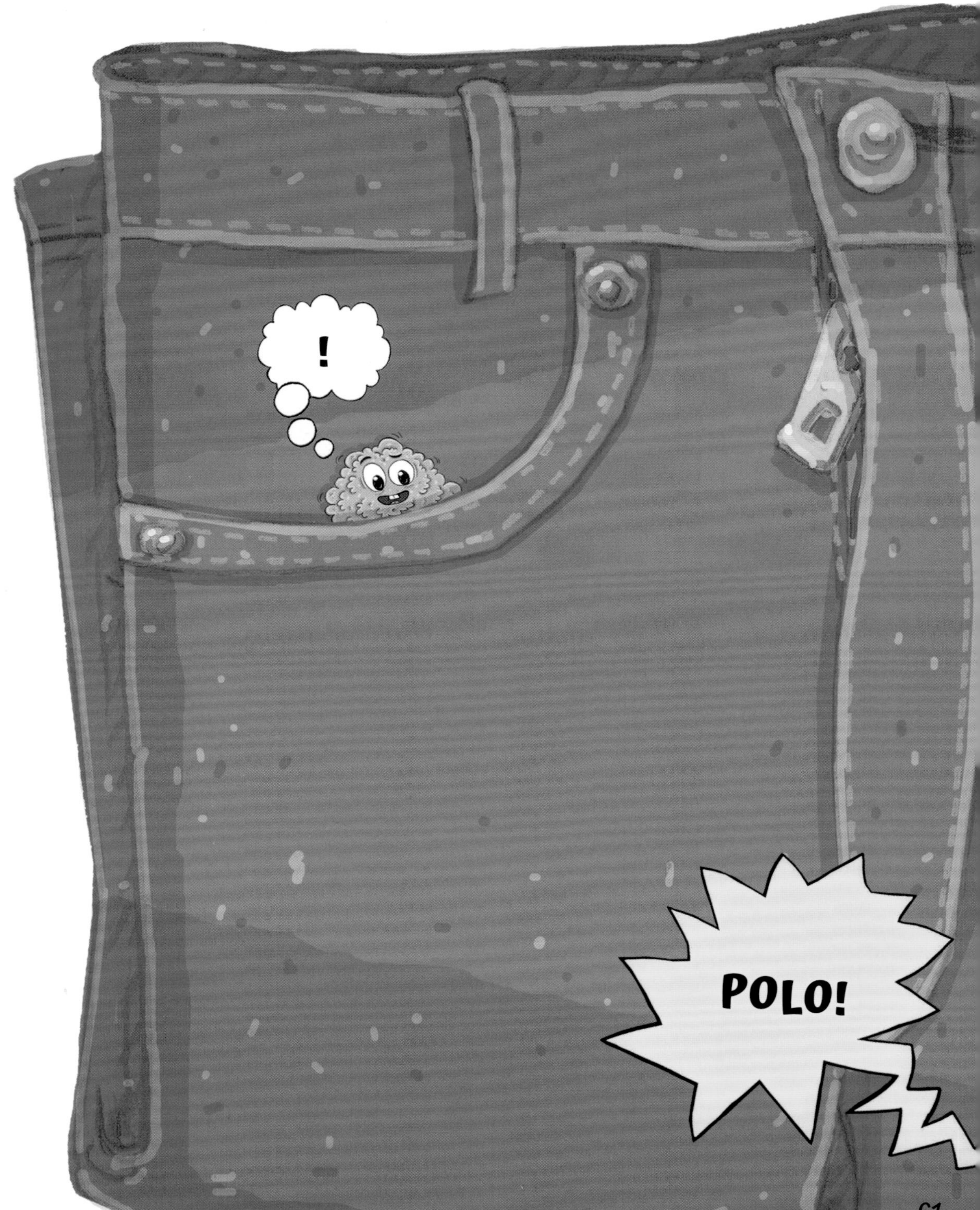
!
POLO!

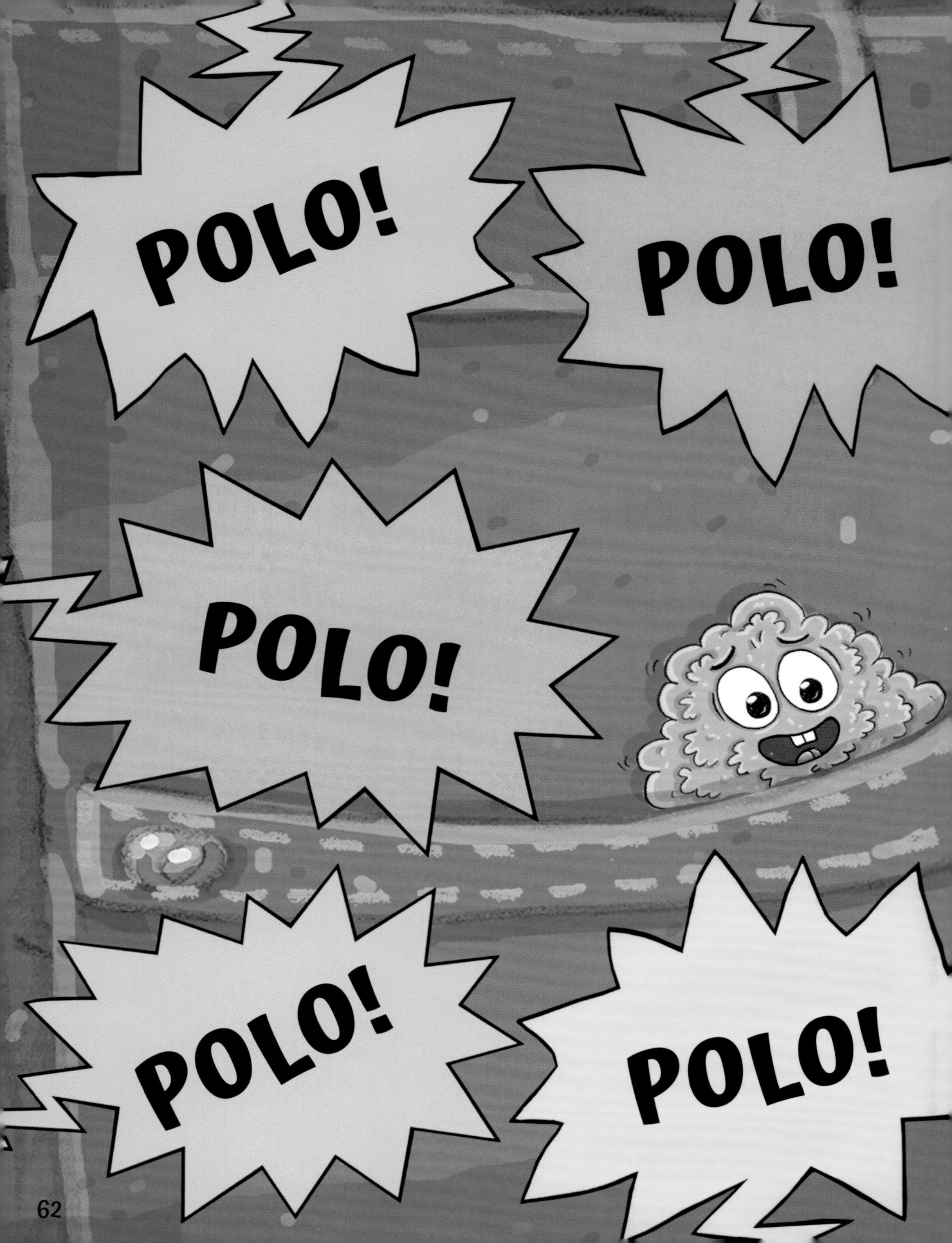
POLO!
POLO!
POLO!
POLO!
POLO!

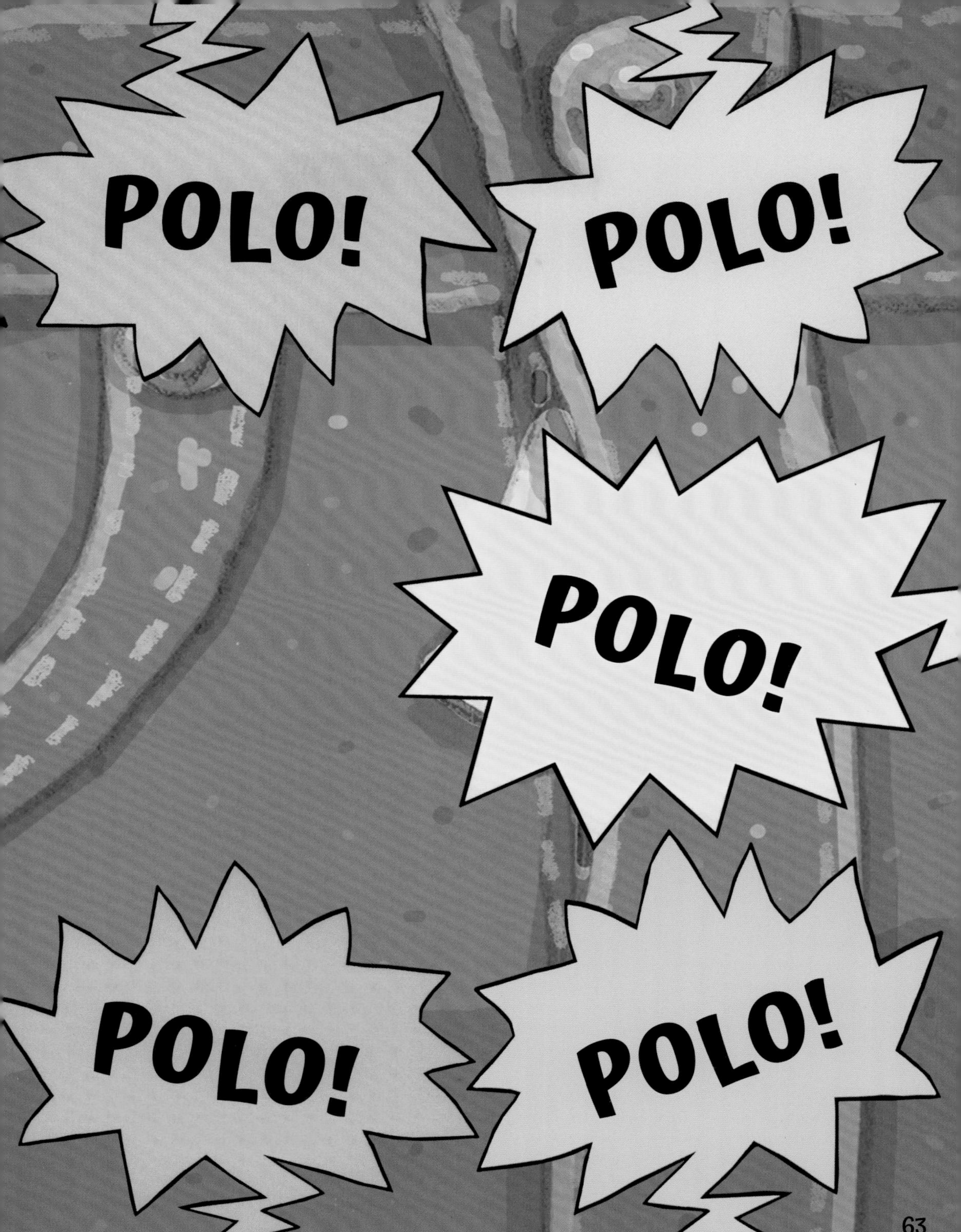
POLO!
POLO!
POLO!
POLO!
POLO!

AND THAT'S WHEN LINTY REALIZED THAT HIS DAYS WOULD NOW BE FILLED WITH NEW ADVENTURES DAY AFTER DAY ...

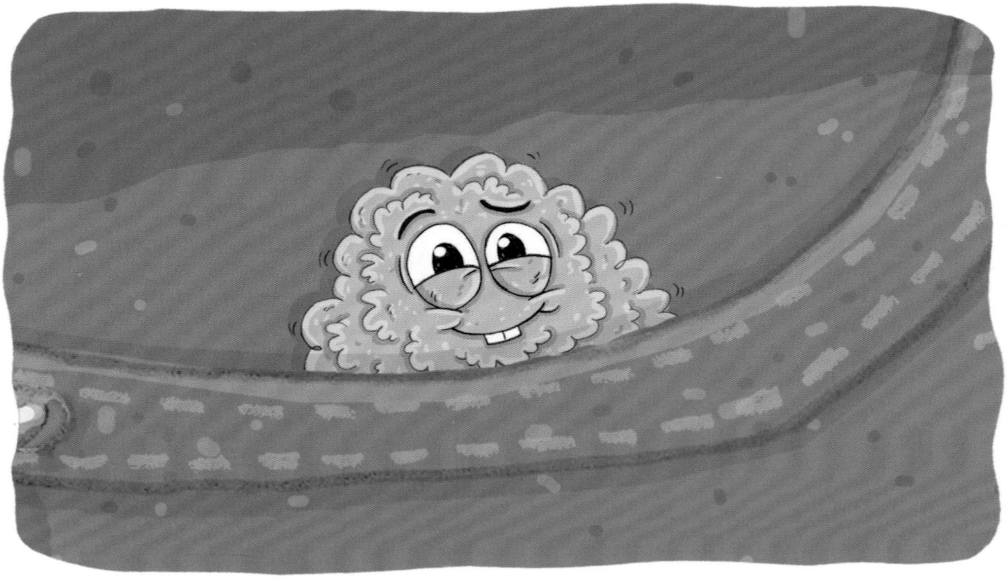

AFTER DAY AFTERDAYAFTERDAY ... (WELL, YOU GET THE POINT.) BUT FIRST ...

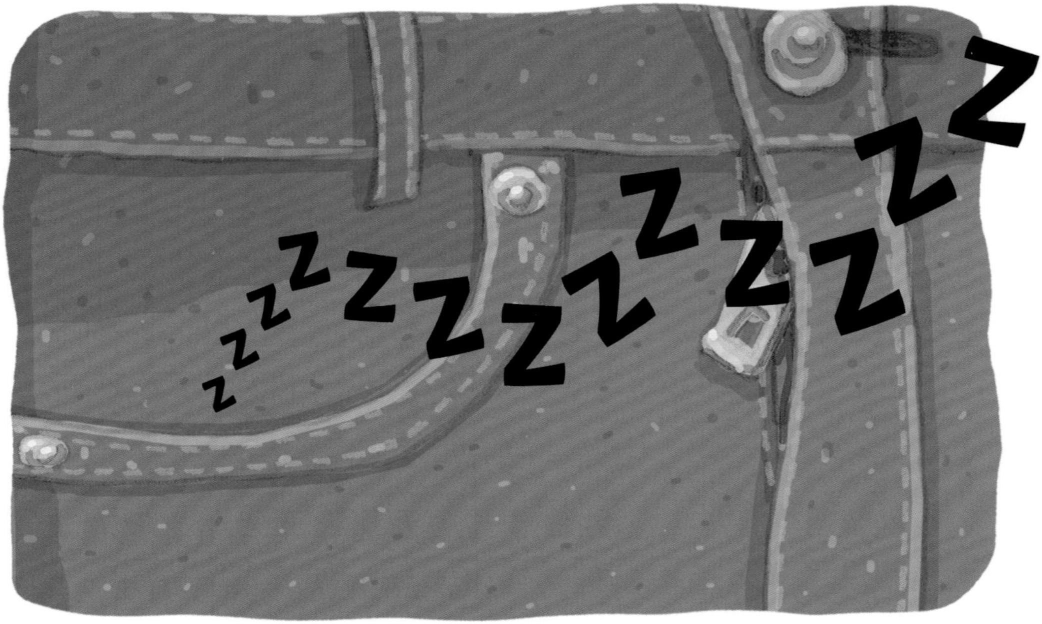
zzzzZZZZZZZZZ